———————— ★ ————————

Deedra panicked, smothered a scream that would have alerted Ricardo and Hannah, and for a century-long time they simply stared at each other.

Then in an unexpected movement, the man gathered her under his arm and quickly reentered the cellar, clattering down the cement steps. He carried her effortlessly. When she wriggled, he clasped her closer to him. She dared not struggle, fearing that he might crush her to death, even though he carried her loosely and only tightened his grip when Deedra struggled.

She saw that the stairwell walls were covered in dark lichen and moss. They entered a large cavern illuminated by a light from the filthy windows under Ricardo's lab. Close to the walls, spider webs festooned from ceiling to floor. The smell of carrion that hung in the air caused bile to rise in her mouth.

A new spurt of fear shot through her at the sight of a large skeleton stretched out on a trundle bed. It was completely covered with spider webs.

The man went to the bed and stared down at the skeleton, tears filling his bleary eyes.

"Da," he mumbled. He pushed aside some of the spider webs with his free hand and patted the skeleton affectionately causing the bones to creak.

———————— ★ ————————

DOROTHY KLIEWER

THE
AWFUL ABBEY

WORLDWIDE®

TORONTO • NEW YORK • LONDON
AMSTERDAM • PARIS • SYDNEY • HAMBURG
STOCKHOLM • ATHENS • TOKYO • MILAN
MADRID • WARSAW • BUDAPEST • AUCKLAND

Recycling programs
for this product may
not exist in your area.

THE AWFUL ABBEY

A Worldwide Mystery/September 2010

First published by Hilliard & Harris.

ISBN-13: 978-0-373-26723-1

Printed in U.S.A.

Dorothy's children are the joy of her life, each of their triumphs has been balm to her heart, and to those dear ones, Bill, Jerry, Debby, Heidi, Joshua, Shiloh, Noah... and Frank, Chuck, Bart, Maria, Tony, Jill, Olivia, Brooke, Judi, Traci, Doug, Halle, Chase, and John, this book is dedicated.

And, with fond memories of Billie, Jeff, Scott, Kathleen, Kristen, Drew, and Carrie.

ONE

"DEEDRA, HAVE YOU ever heard of Ricardo Embustero?" Clete Bailey, the editor of the *Daily Spokesman,* asked the investigative reporter seated opposite him.

Deedra Masefield was in her late twenties. She had the reputation of being a good investigative reporter, and at the moment her sea-blue eyes were alert and wary. She sensed that Clete was about to send her out on a story she might not like, though she dared not object until she heard Clete out. The name Ricardo Embustero meant that something might have happened to his famous movie actress wife, Sharlee Devon…and Deedra always avoided the movie star stories. They were mostly puff and pander for the PR they could wrangle from the news media.

"Yes," she answered, and even Clete could hear the reluctance in her tone of voice. "Isn't he that eccentric inventor who married the lovely Sharlee Devon, Hollywood's newest version of a Marilyn Monroe?"

"Yes. Old Ricardo bought that crotchety old Anthea Abbey up in a town called Bermondy. This priory has the reputation of being haunted; empty so long that Ricardo got it at a bargain price. At the time of purchase, he claimed he needed that kind of space for his inventions, and a place far enough away so as not to annoy near neighbors. He also claimed he was going to remodel it so that Sharlee would have her own 'castle.'"

"Why," Deedra interrupted, "is the place supposed to be haunted?"

"Seems an early 20th century resident turned into a serial killer. Can't think of his name at the moment, but he killed his wife and her sister right there in the abbey. He claimed that the ghosts that haunted the place caused him to do it. The abbey evidently had a reputation early on, and had been empty for twenty or thirty years. You know what happens to old, empty structures. And especially that one. It looks like it was transported here from medieval times. It's got a wicked reputation. The killer was supposed to have hacked up the women's bodies and strung parts of them all over the place."

"Old Ricardo Embustero wasn't afraid to take his beautiful bride to a place like that?" Deedra wondered why Sharlee Devon had ever agreed to it.

Clete grinned. "Well, there are those who said he took Sharlee away from the competition. He ain't all that young, you know, and Hollywood is full of young and virile men," he said.

Deedra giggled. "Yeah, as I recall he isn't the most

handsome man Sharlee ever saw either." The tinkle of her amused laughter echoed around the office.

Clete chuckled. As usual Deedra's humor was infectious. He knew, however, that she was skeptical of this assignment, and he was slightly hesitant about giving it to her.

"What's up?" she challenged.

"Hear me out, Deedra. I think there's something that needs investigating here…a real life mystery."

Deedra sighed. "Aren't they all? Tell me more."

"Here's the file on old Ricardo, tells about his whirlwind courtship with Sharlee Devon and what's happened since they married. I think you'll probably recall most of it anyway. It certainly made news. Now," Clete shifted in his chair and leaned forward as if he was imparting confidential information. "The word is that no one has seen or heard from Sharlee since they finished remodeling and moving into the abbey itself. Ricardo keeps people away, says Sharlee is mentally ill. At least, that's the story he told the local sheriff. Not only that, in these last few months there have been rumors of strange 'goings on' at the awful abbey. Talk about some kind of monster man, that kind of thing."

"Hey, hold on, Clete! Where there are movie stars there is gossip. Perhaps this is just a publicity stunt to get Sharlee back in the mainstream. Maybe she wants to make another picture, and no one has offered!"

"Not true. It's the directors and producers from tinsel-town that are making all these inquiries. A lot of important people in the movie industry are worried about Sharlee. One producer has a film he wants her to star in and he can't get in touch with her. For someone like Sharlee Devon who led a free-style life, that's really strange…and even a little frightening."

Deedra grinned. "So what's happened now to spur you into action?"

Clete leaned forward putting both elbows on his desk, a sure sign that the story was important.

"A young boy delivering newspapers found a note tied to a rock in the driveway of the abbey. Evidently it had been thrown there out of an upstairs window. On the note was written, HELP, S.D. Those are Sharlee's initials. The youngster claims he saw Sharlee at an upstairs window as he rode his bicycle up the driveway. She motioned to the note and then vanished. After he left the paper on the porch, he picked up the note and rode away. He gave the note to the editor of the Bermondy Scribe, who in turn showed it to the sheriff."

"And?" Deedra prompted.

"The sheriff prowled around the place. Ricardo made certain that the sheriff saw Sharlee at an upstairs window. Not having a warrant and no evidence of a crime, the sheriff left. Obviously Ricardo hasn't done away with her, he's just holding her...ah...in-communicado. Why?"

Deedra felt the stirrings of a new investigative-type story. "Go on," she prompted.

"The editor called me, a young man named R.D. Spenser. He had heard that you solved that Rachel Coleridge thing. He thinks this is just as mysterious, and even more dangerous, if I heard him right. Since the sheriff's hands are tied, he thinks a woman might be able to inveigle Ricardo into an interview. You might get into that house, might even have a chance to talk to Sharlee."

"You mean there's a man that thinks a woman might be able to do something they can't?" Deedra sneered. "Oh, sorry about that, Clete. I haven't exactly had a good day."

"Ricardo likes women, Deedra, and sometimes men will do something for a woman they wouldn't for a man. Now, we at the paper here all know that you aren't one of the weaker sex, you've proved that time and time again. But women do have appeal to men. It's a chemistry thing, you know. And you can't tell me that you women don't revel in it."

"I'm not sure I find your last statement a compliment, but I asked for it. I guess that means you want me to go up to Bermondy and find out what gives with Sharlee Devon?"

"Right." Clete leaned back in his chair with the air

of someone who has just completed a difficult task. His manner, however, suggested that there might be something else involved in his wanting to get Deedra out of town.

"Oh, God, don't tell me Daryl Walters is back in town?" she challenged.

Clete nodded. "He's due back tomorrow. I don't want you to be in your office when he arrives."

"Can't you just arrange for some other newspaper to requisition his services?"

Clete shook his head. "No other paper wants him even though he writes with such fervor. I can't fire him, no grounds. He knows that, and he knows that I know it. He never goofs up an assignment, and never misses a deadline."

Deedra sighed. "I'll leave right after lunch." She took the files on Ricardo Embustero, and retreated to her office, thankful that she would be away from her nemesis, Daryl Walters. Daryl pestered her continually with his proposals of marriage. She was not in love with him and did not even like him. He was an extremely capable news reporter, however, and in that capacity she had a certain admiration for his discernment. Daryl was under the impression that persistence would finally win out. That fact made it just the right time for her to get away from the city.

The files on Ricardo were thick. He was eccentric and arrogant with a history for news making. He had invented innumerable things. Some were used in the nuclear and computer fields. He felt he hadn't been properly reimbursed for some of them. His attorney had sued. And at the time he married Sharlee Devin he was described as "filthy rich."

Ricardo had married several women whom he had either divorced or buried. For various reasons, he had escaped paying alimony, claiming to have invented things after the divorces.

Sharlee Devon was a different wife, an out of character-type for him. Sharlee was worth millions in her own right, and was also very beautiful. A category none of his past wives had fit into, though several months earlier rumors circulated among the Hollywood crowd that Sharlee wanted out of the marriage. It was no real surprise. Everyone had expected to see Sharlee emerge from isolation and start a new film. Rejoin the glittery Hollywood scene. But it had not happened. Now, several influential people wanted to know why. What had happened to her and why couldn't they get in touch with her?

Deedra sat back in her chair. Had Sharlee's act of throwing out a note for help been merely a publicity stunt? One really never knew with some of the Hollywood types. But instinct told her that if Sharlee could have left that marriage she would have done so by this time. There was something wrong. No woman of Sharlee's temperament would stand for being kept in an old, cold mausoleum like that unless they couldn't get away.

Whatever. It was a good excuse for Deedra to get away from Daryl Walters. He was always overly pretentious whenever he returned from an assignment, and practically slathered over her desk in his gladness to see her again. She couldn't stand the man and always felt utterly disgusted at his declarations of love and promises of eternal devotion.

She went out to lunch, finished writing several news articles, and then went home to pack.

Bermondy was located sixty miles to the north of them and eighty miles inland from the ocean. This was a land of deep arroyos and jagged scarps, thus not greatly populated. She hated turning inland from the ocean. Deedra had the idea that coastal living was the only way. Although she soon found the area intriguing with the hillsides covered with eucalyptus, cottonwoods, and ancient oak trees all surrounded by chaparral. A river crashed through the ravine, ending in a quiet lake just outside Bermondy. Actually, the town was in a beautiful region despite its location away from the ocean.

The newspaper office was located in one of the more modern buildings in the quaint town and she had no trouble locating it. Bermondy had grown up after World War I, its buildings reminiscent of that era. But it was charming. It had its own aura and Deedra found it pleasant.

She entered the newspaper office, a place still clinging to the town's early décor, and smiled to herself. This weekly newspaper had sustained its readership in spite of all the encroachments of modern day technology and daily newspapers from San Francisco.

R.D. Spenser, a young man with glasses perched on his nose, was seated behind a desk near the window so he could watch the street and the town's activity.

Deedra introduced herself.

R.D. Spenser stood up and shook her outstretched hand. He was a young thirty-five and wore glasses that shielded his shrewd eyes. He was thin and bookish-looking. As editor and publisher of the Bermondy Scribe, he obviously felt pride in that fact.

"This is Kortney Vickers, one of our reporters and the clerical person here. Between us, and old Roger Manning, who runs the computer set-up, we manage to get out a weekly newspaper."

Kortney Vickers had an energetic attractiveness and regarded Deedra with obvious envy. It lurked in her green eyes, making Deedra aware that Kortney was disenchanted with small town life. She was probably saving for the day when she could leave the boring social news of Bermondy for a chance on some big city newspaper.

R.D. offered her a chair opposite his desk and poured her a cup of excellent coffee. "I'll fill you in on what's happened here," he said as he took a seat and leaned back in his chair. "One of our newspaper delivery boys found this note," he handed her a crumpled piece of paper, "which was thrown onto the driveway of the abbey from an upstairs window just as he was riding his bicycle up the driveway. The boy saw Sharlee Devon at the window. She put a finger over her lips to indicate silence and then disappeared. Curt Ralston, the delivery boy, left just as fast as he could get away. That's a creepy old place at best. There's nothing friendly or inviting about it and it takes real guts just to deliver the papers there. We're all hoping that old Ricardo didn't see the boy pick up the note."

R.D. sipped his coffee and began again. "Now, Sharlee Devon was right friendly when they first arrived here. That was when the abbey was being remodeled, if you can call it that. Then right after they moved into the abbey itself, everything changed. She never leaves the place; is never seen here in town. It's as if old Ricardo keeps her hostage there. And he won't let her have visitors, chases everyone away."

R.D. paused, sipped coffee. "Now, if you remember, Sharlee was always giving interviews previous to her move here and has appeared on several talk shows. This is a complete change of character. No one really knows if she's ill, if she's really dead, or if Ricardo has someone pretending to be her who is showing up at those upstairs windows just long enough for a glimpse. She's never there long enough for a positive I.D. No one has seen her up close or talked to her in months and months. But this note indicates that she probably is alive and needs help. We're duty bound to find out why."

He paused again, studying her, wanting to see her reaction. "I've had innumerable requests from Hollywood wanting information about Sharlee. I can't supply them with any kind of satisfactory explanation about why they aren't able to contact her. Most of them think Ricardo is afraid of losing her and prevents her from seeing any of her old friends. And that is about what it amounts to—she is prevented in some way from contacting people. Now, with all this wife battering and abuse publicity, people are beginning to really worry."

Deedra nodded. "How would you suggest that I get in to see Sharlee?"

R.D. smiled. "I've thought and thought about how to manage that. Ricardo is suspicious of everyone. He claims people are out to steal his inventions, and I guess some inventors have a paranoia about that. I think if you go there, tell him you're a reporter from a big city newspaper, flatter him about his inventions, tell him you would like to write a story about him being one of the most honored inventors of the 20th century. Tell him that he is very intelligent and that the public needs to know that. Make a pitch to photo his laboratory where he puts his genius to work. My goodness, what a thrill for a lowly reporter like yourself! You want to remember that Ricardo is not averse to a pretty, sexy lady."

Deedra giggled. "I'm to play the silly female?"

"Yeah," R.D. grinned.

"It might work. I'm not an actress, though. Still, I've had to play roles in the past. I suppose I could try to out-vamp old Ricardo. I think flattery would work best, though. Do you think he would be interested in me as a woman?"

"If he's tired of Sharlee. He's an often-married man, which indicates that he can't go very long without the companionship of a female. Or that he likes various types."

"Thanks loads! Just how am I to compete with Sharlee?" Deedra thought of another rude comment, but kept it to herself. "What do you really think is going on up there? Your honest undiluted opinion."

R.D. glanced out the window, obviously deep in contemplation. It was several moments before he answered. "I think Ricardo is insane. There've been rumors of a monster up there, a human that has grown into something very ugly. Things have happened to people who have gone out on that road after dark. At first it was thought to be the imagination of the people who told of their experiences close to the abbey that were taken in by the abbey's evil reputation. Now, I'm not sure. Ricardo is an inventor and he could easily be playing scary tricks to frighten people away. I think Ricardo lives on borderline reality; that he has delved into some kind of wicked experiments. It isn't normal for a man to keep his wife a virtual prisoner. Especially a world-famous actress. If Sharlee were a different type, if she really hated being in the public eye, then it wouldn't seem so strange. But the fact that Ricardo keeps her from her friends, and from the adulation that she clearly thrived on, is pure cruelty."

Deedra nodded. "Tell me how to get out there. And please remember where I've gone in case I fail to return."

R.D. gave her the directions. "It's a huge old place. Reminds me of medieval Europe with its castles and dungeons. The grounds are rank with overgrowth, trailing vines, that kind of thing. All of which adds to its spookiness. We had a heck of a time trying to get a boy brave enough to deliver the paper out there. Curt Ralston is something of a hero here in Bermondy. The only boy brave enough to deliver the newspaper to the awful abbey."

"You call it that, too? Clete Bailey referred to it as the awful abbey."

"Got that name from the time murders were

committed there. You can imagine what a terrible thing that was, those bodies all cut up, blood everywhere."

"Has the story of those old murders been revived lately? That maybe the old stories fueled the new rumors?

"No. I haven't printed anything and none of the daily papers we get here have."

"Perhaps the fact that Sharlee hasn't been seen gives people a chance to gossip. You know how people like to talk about movie stars and public figures. Sometimes people even make up things to talk about. Perhaps part of this is just talk."

R.D. nodded. "You'll have to see for yourself. But a word of caution, just be very careful not to let Ricardo know your real reason for going there. Keep flattering him, keep telling him how smart you think he is."

When R.D. noted her skepticism, he asked, "Do you know Chuck Preston, the news anchor?"

"Yes."

"Preston spent a weekend at the abbey. He told me he's never been so frightened in his whole life."

"Chuck Preston was frightened there, and admitted it?" Deedra felt a shiver clamber over her body. If Chuck Preston was afraid of that place, then there really was something unusual going on. She decided to call Preston and learn first hand what happened during his visit to Anthea Abbey.

TWO

THE DRIVE TO the old abbey seemed unreal, as if she was going through a scene in a scary movie. Trees overshadowed twisting narrow lanes; strange mists clung to the dark green foliage and hovered in shallow glens. Where no trees grew, chaparral festered along the roadsides. Like a serpent, the road wended in and around following the river on one side and a deep ravine on the other. A wide bridge straddled the ravine, and when she neared the abbey she crossed a narrow archaic bridge. It was so old she had to drive carefully to keep from scraping the sides, reflecting on the fact that the Model T's of that era were nothing more than automated buggies.

Once across the bridge, she stopped to gaze at the huge structure jutting into the sky above the trees. It was constructed of gray stones, medieval-like in appearance, and sprawled over a slight knoll. The grounds were thickly overgrown. Twining vines clutched at gnarled trees whose moss-laden limbs almost touched the ground. The road ended at the driveway into the abbey.

"One way in and one way out," she muttered, then turned the car into the driveway.

The priory loomed before her like a stark mausoleum, its gloomy facade enhanced by erosion of the grayish granite, pitted and filled with pervasive lichen. It hunched there like a sleeping gargoyle. The vines that cluttered the grounds resembled serpents slithering among trees and shrubs. There was something ghoulish about it and she couldn't believe that Ricardo had the nerve to bring his famous wife to such a place.

It had such a malevolent aura, a mien of melancholy, and a depressive spirit with an essence of chill foreboding. It was as if the abbey had no inner spark. No wonder R.D. said they had trouble getting anyone to deliver papers out here. Only the strong of mind would even attempt it.

The old abbey definitely had a reptilian look.

Deedra shuddered.

After calming herself, she drove on down the drive aware that whoever lurked within was probably alerted to her presence.

As she got out of the car, a rapid movement like the flutter of a wild bird attracted her attention to a window on the top floor. A pale female face peered out, then vanished.

It happened so quickly Deedra was not certain she had really seen a woman standing there. That part of the abbey was an appendage, like an after-thought. From its outward appearance, it didn't appear to be part of the main house. Then she realized that it was a turret, an addition made to resemble a tower.

The cobblestone steps showed no wear, no indication of their ancient age. She experienced a creepy feeling as she climbed the stairs. Thoughts of this old place being haunted jarred her imagination. The doorknocker resounded loudly, echoing through the interior. No one could miss hearing it. However, silence followed its summons. It was several minutes before the clatter of footsteps, hurried mincing footsteps, stopped just before reaching the door.

"Stay back!" a sharp command.

"Oh!" a female wail.

The heavy door screeched open, its echo ricocheting up a dark hall. She glimpsed wide stairs on each side of the hall separating the house into dim labyrinths leading to its pith and marrow.

The tall man who stepped into the doorway was surprising. Strands of white streaked his raven-colored black hair causing a stripe effect reminiscent of an animal.

Deedra forced her attention from the man's hair to his eyes…and experienced a shock. His eyes were deep pools of malice. He stared at her with belligerence and obvious hostility.

After a moment of suspicious inspection, he

growled, "State your business, young lady! I haven't time to stand here all day."

Deedra found herself babbling. "I'm Deedra Masefield of the *Daily Spokesman*. I'd like to write a feature story on your inventions, Mr. Embustero. I know you're a genius, and I think people would be interested in knowing about the things you've invented. Are you inventing something now that you could tell the readers about? I understand many of the things you've invented have helped the government in both the computer and outer space fields." Deedra paused to catch her breath.

Ricardo Embustero just stared at her.

Seeing that she had made no impression on him, she went on. "You see, I need a big story to get a promotion at the newspaper. It means a raise, too, and that's kind of essential for a single gal like me. I just thought a really intelligent person like you could provide an intriguing story that my editor would like and print." Deedra fluttered her eyelids, tilted her head to one side in what she thought was a feminine wile. She really didn't understand what a feminine wile was, but she gave it a fling.

Ricardo continued staring, but something moved in the stygian depths of his dark eyes. It was not at all reassuring. Finally, Ricardo moved to one side and bowed her into the house. Almost, she thought, like the spider to the fly. The look on his face was mocking, humorless.

Deedra was suddenly aware of a woman in the shadows of the staircase. The woman placed a finger over her lips then melded into deeper shadow. Deedra recognized Sharlee Devon, a frail ethereal version of the beautiful movie actress. If this house was truly haunted, then Sharlee was a ghost of her former self, and with that thought, fear for Sharlee sent a shudder down her spine.

Ricardo Embustero led her down the long hall where he opened a door to a large laboratory that was so huge it ran the full length of the house. Heavy draperies covered the windows. Ricardo turned on a light above a workbench littered with chemicals, powders, glass tubes, old Bunsen burners and other unrecognizable paraphernalia. Half-finished inventions were placed everywhere.

Several partitions had obviously been removed to create the lab. It was the clutter of it that struck Deedra as strange. Nothing seemed to have a sense of order or organization. The equipment and lab tools were helter-skelter, though two computers occupied a bench-like desk, their screens flickering with screen savers.

If Ricardo kept such a close watch on Sharlee, how did he spend any time on inventions? Ricardo answered that himself by turning on a surveillance camera that viewed Sharlee Devon pacing the length of the upstairs hall.

Deedra felt as if she had been stabbed with a knife of ice. What kind of man would do such a thing to his wife? She sensed the danger and struggled to control her fear and anger.

Ricardo turned off the camera. "My wife," he smiled, "is not well. I keep an eye on her to prevent her from…ah…hurting herself." The villainous smile sought her understanding.

Deedra managed to smile and nod.

Fortunately Ricardo didn't question her, and went on explaining some of his inventions.

It was all very boring, but Deedra took copious notes, straining for sounds that would indicate someone lingered in the hallway.

She prompted Ricardo with hints about his unique intelligence. He went on and on in self-aggrandizement for a time before turning on the monitor again.

Sharlee was still in the upstairs hall looking out a window that faced the front of the abbey.

Ricardo once again switched the monitor off and turned to her with a bland smile.   Deedra struggled with disgust and fear. She muttered something meant to sound sympathetic, but was actually a curse on him.

Ricardo relaxed. He evidently believed he had persuaded her that he was a concerned husband, wanting only to protect his "ill" wife.

Egotists, Deedra mused, were easy to fool, but Ricardo had a cruel streak and was definitely dangerous. R.D. hadn't been out of line to caution her.

Deedra wanted to ask questions about Sharlee but sensed that would give away her purpose in being there. She needed to leave with the idea that Ricardo might allow her to visit again and didn't want him to exert his spleen on Sharlee after she was gone.

She dared not hurry Ricardo with his explanations. Some of the inventions were quite interesting, though he was vague about several of them as if he didn't quite understand their function himself. He always avoided her questions about anything in progress. Did he think her too dull to understand their function, or was he too paranoid to explain the details?

When at last they emerged from the laboratory, Deedra had the sensation of escaping from something dire and couldn't prevent the shudder that skimmed her spine.

As they walked up the long hall, Deedra peered into the shadows hoping for another glimpse of Sharlee.

She couldn't believe they had actually remodeled the abbey. It was certainly no tribute to the decorator. Deedra suspected that Ricardo hadn't really hired anyone except the carpenters. The walls were bereft of

color, painted a dull dungeon color. The whole place
lacked any suggestion of warmth. A few splotches of
color would have relieved some of that cold dungeon
look. There weren't even any pictures on the walls
and she wondered what had happened to Sharlee's
collection of famous paintings.

"How many rooms are there here in the abbey?"
she asked.

Ricardo halted in his long stride toward the front
door. Finally he replied in a tone as cold as the
house.

"I am not sure. I haven't really paid attention since
the abbey was remodeled. We took out partitions,
added things here and there. It has three floors and
that octagonal turret my wife calls her own. I let her
roam there, and perhaps she imagines it's a movie set.
That part was not remodeled. I didn't intend to make
use of it." He smiled that villain smile. "That's where
all the ghostly activity is supposed to take place."

Deedra felt a start of surprise. "I wasn't aware of
any ghostly activity!"

"Well," he smiled again, "there seems to be rumors
of such and, of course, the abbey has had a haunted
reputation for years and years."

"You bought it knowing that?" When he nodded
she remarked, "How about that."

She went out through the front door Ricardo was
holding open. "Oh, do you mind if I wander about

these beautiful grounds? I'll be able to describe them better if I do." She smiled her most sexy smile again.

Ricardo responded with permission. "Of course. You understand that since I am involved with a new invention, I haven't given the grounds the attention they obviously need."

Deedra nodded her thanks, refraining from asking why he didn't hire a gardener or landscape person to clean them up. Lack of money couldn't be the excuse.

She scurried down the steps, taking in gulps of fresh air and feeling as if she had escaped from some medieval dungeon.

Ricardo's voice halted her. "If you care to add to your feature article, I shall have another invention completed in a few weeks. The patent is applied for. It should give you what you people call a scoop."

"Why, thank you!" Words failed her. She just kept smiling until he closed the heavy door.

Sharlee was at the front window staring toward her car, she looked at Deedra, then at the car again. Then she vanished behind heavy draperies.

Deedra walked toward her car and saw a rock with paper tied around it. Sharlee had evidently thrown out another note. It was just out of Ricardo's sight. He couldn't see it from his place at the front window.

Instead of picking up the note, she walked on

toward a path of multicolored pebbles that meandered between rampant growing ivy tendrils. The tendrils clung in a lecherous way to every tree and shrub. They were heavy and in some places sagged to the ground, bringing the tree branches to the ground. The path ended at a large pool where an early European style fountain stood in silent splendor. The fountain figure was that of a woman gracefully pouring water from a heavy jar. The lecherous vines covered her, and the tendrils looped into the stagnant water. Wisteria vines twisted around several other trees and shrubs.

Deedra walked down another path that ended at an old summerhouse. From there she saw another building, which she later learned was an art studio. Though she prowled among the rancid growth for several minutes, she didn't see any movement from the turret windows. Hiding behind heavy foliage she could see the abbey unobserved. How would, she wondered, they ever get Sharlee out of that gloomy old mausoleum?

For several minutes she studied the gray structure with its ashen-colored stones, the lichen creeping ever upward. Just the sight of it was enough to bring the word "haunted" to her mind. It was definitely the most forbidding and foreboding place Deedra had ever seen. It exuded vibes that made her think there were festerings going on within its dreary walls.

THREE

AT LAST HER vigilance was rewarded when Deedra saw Sharlee peek out the window at the far right of the turret. Sharlee was obviously going to watch to see if Deedra picked up the note.

When Deedra emerged from the tangled foliage she noted that Ricardo was still standing at the downstairs front window. She knew he was probably watching her like a vulture did its prey. She turned and went back through the twisting of undergrowth to the pond, skirted it, then stopped beneath a gnarled oak tree whose dangling vines dripped into the stagnant pond.

She rested a few moments and just stared into the pond, absorbing the isolation of this spooky neglected place.

A voice at her side suddenly hissed, "What are you doing here?"

Deedra screamed.

The tall woman who stood in the shadow of the tree with hostility glowing from her dark eyes was holding a shovel in a very threatening way. Never had Deedra seen a woman with such a bulbous nose, a nose that drew attention to the center of this woman's face. There was nothing soft about the woman. She was rawboned and strongly built...and menacing. The old-fashioned long black dress she wore did nothing to reassure Deedra.

"Ah...Mr. Embustero gave me permission to explore the grounds. I'm Deedra Masefield, a reporter for the *Daily Spokesman*. Who are you?"

The old woman stared. She didn't relax her grip on the shovel. "I'm Hannah Embustero. I'm housekeeper here since Ricardo's wife is not...umm...able."

"Are you related to Mr. Embustero then?" Deedra hoped the woman wouldn't notice that she was trembling.

Hannah muttered something under her breath, turned away and hurried along the path leading toward the rear of the house. As she scurried along, her voluminous skirt trailed out behind her and Deedra wouldn't have been surprised if it had lifted her off the ground like a kite. The woman disappeared around a bramble thicket and though Deedra waited, she didn't glimpse the woman who called herself Hannah Embustero again.

The unexpected meeting with Hannah had left her shaken and even more uneasy, causing her chills as she passed dark shadowy places along the path. Eventually she reached a lattice shelter built into a slight knoll as if it had been dug out for that purpose. The steps were of stone and led down to the door located several feet below ground level. Clematis vines covered the exterior and it had obviously not been in use for several years.

Behind this shelter was the deep arroyo, quite close in fact, and Deedra thought it likely that the shelter would erode away into the ravine at some point in the future.

With a hasty glance toward the abbey, whose facade was hidden by foliage, she went down the broken steps. She found the door locked, though there was a slight disturbance of the clematis vines indicating that someone had been there recently. Unable to enter, she went back up the stairs and onto the path that led to the front lawn. All the while she experienced the feeling of being watched and of wondering if Hannah was nearby with her shovel. Or if Ricardo had the grounds under his special type of surveillance. She did nothing but look around, nothing to make him suspicious of her motive for being there. But by the time she reached the front of the abbey she was trembling, and feeling helpless and hopeless. Paranoia did that to a person.

She walked as slowly as she could to the car, circled it, swinging her handbag in a casual way. She stood a moment studying the grounds on the other side of the drive and as Deedra turned back to the car, dropped her handbag beside the note. She stood a moment with her hands on her hips as if in disgust, and then gathered up the note with the items from her handbag.

Without appearing to hurry, she climbed into the car. She spent a moment looking for her keys and allowed the note to drop into her handbag. She glanced toward the turret where Sharlee was nodding her head, then waved at Ricardo and Hannah who stood at the front window.

As she turned the car onto the road she drew a deep breath and released it with a hiss. What a monstrous situation Sharlee had brought on herself by marrying such an egomaniac. Though anxious to read Sharlee's note, she drove across the archaic bridge and around the bend to a place where she could park off the road.

With shaking hands she untied the string around the rock. The note was quite crumpled.

"Help. R.E. prevents me from taking baby outside. Can't leave without him. S.D."

Deedra reread the note in complete astonishment. Never had there been a hint that the famous actress had given birth to a child! So that was how Ricardo controlled her. What a monster he was! The danger to Sharlee was even greater than anyone had imagined. It was almost as if Ricardo lived in medieval times holed up in a cold dungeon of a house with a captive female…and he was the mad scientist!

Again Deedra experienced cold tremors.

Relief flooded through her when the car engine sputtered to life. No way did she want to be stranded anywhere around the abbey. The coldness of her spirit continued until she entered the quaint town with its old buildings and friendly people bustling about the streets. The feeling of dismal uneasiness faded as she parked in front of the newspaper office. People on the street eyed her curiously. Strangers were an item of interest in this small town. However, Deedra mused that there was something to be said for big city anonymity.

R.D. Spenser was conferring with two men dressed in business suits. He shot her a warning glance.

Deedra went to the counter where a stack of news-papers was for sale. She dropped a coin into the pay jar, then went to a chair near the window where she pretended to read the want ads. She couldn't overhear what the men were saying, however.

Kortney Vickers wasn't at her desk.

After a few moments of close inspection, Deedra concluded that the men were law officers, probably F.B.I. men. One of them glanced her way and did a double take as if he thought he should know her, but couldn't quite place her. After a moment of close scrutiny he turned back to the others.

When the men left, R.D. told her why they were in town. "F.B.I. That delivery boy, the one who found the note from Sharlee Devon, is missing. His name is

Curt Ralston and his father owns the bank here. The boy hasn't been home for three days now."

"A search has been made here in Bermondy?" She didn't understand why there hadn't been a concentration of people searching around the abbey.

"There's no sign of him in Bermondy. Curt completed the delivery of The Scribe on Wednesday afternoon and that's the last report of anyone having seen him. I called all the subscribers on his route today. They had all received their newspaper Wednesday. Those that did see him said he didn't seem upset, was as friendly as always, and didn't seem to be in any special hurry. The sheriff has no leads, though has set up search teams to look into the ravine and around the lake. The only clue we have is that the old woman who lives at the edge of town, on the only road leading out of Bermondy, reported that Curt had delivered her paper as usual and talked to her for a few minutes, then turned his bicycle around and rode back into town. His bicycle is also missing."

"Any connection with the note the boy found from Sharlee?"

"I've no idea. The F.B.I. men went out there to question old Ricardo when they left here. I'm just glad you're not in that vicinity now. Ricardo would immediately suspect that you were part of their team and order you off his property."

"I hope they won't tell Ricardo about Curt finding that note!"

"No. They don't believe there's a connection at this point, and the sheriff told them that Ricardo claims that Sharlee is mentally ill. I'm sure Ricardo can convince them of that."

"Just look at this!" She handed R.D. the note Sharlee had thrown onto the drive.

"Baby!" R.D. sounded excited. "No one has ever mentioned a baby! Perhaps she is ill, just imagining things. Otherwise we surely would have been aware that she's had a child."

"Perhaps not. That may be the reason she is being held incommunicado. People have had children in secrecy for many hundreds of years. Hospitals weren't necessarily required," she reminded.

"It's true, the baby has to be less than a year old. No one else has been able to get near Sharlee, and she wasn't pregnant when they moved into the abbey from the art studio on the grounds. Before that, Sharlee was often seen in town. She made a close friend of Sandy Harris, the local doctor's wife. They went everywhere together, had similar interests and backgrounds. Sandy was very hurt when Sharlee suddenly cut off their friendship."

"Oh? When was that?"

R.D. frowned. "Must be about two years ago now. Seems like it was early spring. Sandy went out to the abbey and when Ricardo refused her admittance, she made a scene at the local watering hole, The Nugget. Sandy went on and on about how Ricardo ordered her off his property without even an explanation. Sharlee was seen in town after that, and Sandy was never able to contact her. And Sharlee didn't try to contact Sandy. Finally, Sandy just put her out of her life."

"You say they were both models?"

"Yes, early on in Sharlee's career. I believe that's how she was discovered."

"Models," Deedra remarked, "that probably means they kept up with old acquaintances, agents and directors. Had they planned a movie or something, and Ricardo found out about it?"

R.D. shrugged. "If they did, Sandy never mentioned it."

"There was nothing the sheriff could do?"

"He's made several inquiries. He doesn't like getting those inquiries from Hollywood. It irritates him and points out the hopelessness of starting an investigation without the power of a warrant. Ricardo just tells him that Sharlee is mentally ill. And since the sheriff has seen her at the upstairs window several times, there's no evidence of a crime that would get him a warrant to search the place or talk to Sharlee."

"Not yet, anyway," Deedra challenged. She looked

out the window, then asked, "Any criminal activity going on in this town?"

"Not in Bermondy. There are rumors of an illegal gambling casino up in the mountains east of town on an estate owned by Reuben Zolar. Zolar has the reputation of being a drug dealer, but no one has actually proved that. Once in a while people from his estate buy supplies, lots of supplies, from the businesses and residents here in Bermondy. That keeps the citizens from objecting to the reported gambling up there. The place in on private property, not located in this town, or even in this state. And there haven't been any complaints. Zolar owns a helicopter and evidently that's how he travels in and out of his estate. It's just out of our law enforcement's jurisdiction."

"It's located in Nevada then?" When R.D. nodded she asked, "How far away in Nevada?"

"It's only an hour or so across the mountains by helicopter. There's a rumor that a road has been built up there from the Nevada side. I guess there had to be to get all that heavy construction equipment up there."

"But there is a road to it from this side?"

"Yes, it's located on the far side of the lake and leads into his private home. People just can't go up there any time they want. Zolar has it gated, and permission to enter is very limited."

"Has that led to any trouble?" Deedra asked.

"No."

"Does Zolar own the property on each side of the road into his estate?"

"No. They say the owner is a man from Los Angeles that none of us have ever seen. That he leases the private road to Zolar. But everyone really believes that Zolar is the real owner. Anyway, he effectively keeps people away from his mountain aerie."

"Then you don't think the boy's disappearance could have anything to do with this Zolar person?"

R.D. shook his head.

"No. Zolar doesn't want to call attention to his operation up there. Besides, the boy's father isn't really rich. He does own the bank, and is more wealthy than the average citizen, but he's far from being wealthy enough for someone to demand a hefty ransom."

"He might be able to get ransom money though?"

"I suppose. I don't know much about banking practices. I just know that they haven't received a ransom note and I don't think they will, either. I don't think anyone from up here kidnapped Curt. He was either taken by a pedophile or he's in the area somewhere. I wouldn't bet against the notion that he's somewhere in or around the abbey."

"Since there's no ransom note and no indication that the boy was kidnapped, why is the F.B.I. here?"

"The father insists that the boy has been kidnapped

and contacted them himself. He insists that the boy would never just stay away from home unless he was prevented from doing so. I'm certain that is true. Curt is a very dependable boy and has never caused his parents grief. The father is upset because he hasn't received a ransom note. Told me if he had, he could be sure the boy was alive."

"Has the F.B.I. told him that it doesn't always mean anything, that by the time the victims receive a ransom note the child is usually dead?" She glanced out the window. "It would indicate what has happened to him though. I'm with you, I think Curt was up around the abbey and was caught there. That old Hannah is quite capable of anything. And let me tell you, when she stood there holding that shovel, I had visions of her using it to clobber me. And that she had just used it to bury something."

"Hannah? Who is Hannah?"

"You mean you don't know there's this long-nosed old woman who wears a voluminous black dress lurking around the abbey? She says her name is Hannah Embustero. I guess she must be Ricardo's sister or something. She told me she was there to keep house since Sharlee isn't able to."

"I've never heard of the woman. I've never heard anyone mention a woman living at the abbey. How on earth did you happen to meet her?"

She told R.D. of Hannah's sudden appearance. "I

tell you, R.D., it was like I walked into some ancient scene in medieval times. She was this very tall woman whose piercing black eyes glowed like coals. She has a nose you'd have to see to really understand why it dominates her face. And that long old dress she wears trails out behind her like a kite."

"So she's the basis for some of these rumors about the place being haunted?" R.D. was so surprised the pupils of his eyes enlarged behind his glasses.

Deedra nodded. "I'm certain she is. And she would certainly try to give that impression to anyone who met her in the dark anywhere near the abbey. In that black dress she could easily be mistaken for one of the nuns who resided there a century ago. A nun-ghost."

"Hm." R.D. frowned. "But you did see Sharlee?"

"Yes. She was in the shadows on the stairs when I first went inside, then later she stood looking down from the turret window. Sharlee looked from me to the note, and then back again. Then she disappeared. I guess she didn't dare point because of that damn surveillance monitoring."

"What?" Again R.D. seemed startled.

Then Deedra had to explain about Ricardo's surveillance monitoring and how she had seen Sharlee pacing the rooms of the turret on the monitoring screen. "Can you imagine that? The man has an unusually cruel character."

R.D. sighed. "Yes. And I think Ricardo knows exactly what has happened to Curt Ralston," R.D. replied and ran a hand over his eyes. He seemed to feel responsible, at least in part, for Curt's disappearance.

Deedra wondered if R.D. had told them all he knew about the people and happenings at the spooky old abbey.

FOUR

R.D. ASKED MORE QUESTIONS about Hannah, still puzzled that anyone could live up at the abbey and had never been seen there. "How do we know there aren't others in there then? The place is large enough...ah... to hold a convent!"

"Believe me, R.D., Hannah is there all right. She dresses drearily and her manner is as gloomy as the decor." She went on to explain what the abbey was like and how it lacked any trace of color, how dismal and desolate its atmosphere.

"I still can't believe that no one has reported seeing her!" R.D. had trouble with the realization that he didn't hear or know about everything that went on in Bermondy.

"I just think people have seen her and reported it as one of the strange goings-on or thought she was a ghost and were reluctant to admit to seeing such a thing." Deedra paused a moment. "Tell me about the abbey. Why was it built there, and since it was obviously a cloister, why isn't it used for that purpose now? What happened to the nuns that were there years ago?"

"The abbey was constructed by the Cistercians around 1880 on a medieval architectural plan with basements and sub-cellars." R.D. enthusiastically launched into a tale about the history of the old abbey. "The cellars, I understand, are just as they were in those days, though perhaps they are boarded up now. I know the construction people doing the remodeling thought the cost to redo them was prohibitive. One of the guys working there said they were just 'damn scary' and thought Ricardo a little mad for buying the old place."

R.D. poured himself a cup of coffee and gestured to Deedra to help herself.

"Anyway, it was called Anthea Abbey, some say they took the name from the Mother Superior at that time. A cloister of Cistercian nuns settled there shortly after the abbey was completed. No one seems to know exactly what happened to the nuns or why they suddenly left. Only a few were alive in 1910. Evidently they didn't take in any new recruits. That left the abbey vacant for a number of years. Then an oil millionaire, who wanted to turn it into a museum for his art collection and archaeological items brought back from around the world, purchased it. I understand that he had some remodeling done at that time. But since it had been an old abbey and was a good example of medieval European architecture, he didn't want to change the basic structure. He did turn the abbot's house into an art studio, which is where Ricardo and Sharlee lived when the remodeling they initiated went on. The washhouse was turned into a summerhouse. When the millionaire lost all of his money in the crash of 1929, he killed himself. It was the first tragedy there."

R.D. took a sip of coffee. "The abbey was vacant for several years after that. It went through probate, then into the possession of the man who killed his wife and sister-in-law there. He obtained possession of the abbey because the oilman had owed him money and it was all he could collect from him after the crash. It's not known what brought on his fit of rage that resulted in the death of the women. A servant witnessed it and ran to Bermondy with the terrible news. The servant ended up in a mental institution. The bodies were hacked up, you know, and left strewn about the abbey. The servant had hidden on the turret stairs, obviously too frightened to move, until the insane man went off to another part of the abbey. Screaming with the terror of it, the servant ran out the front door and by the time he reached Bermondy, he was in such a state it was difficult to understand what he was saying."

He took another sip of coffee. "The people here knew that something terrible had happened at the abbey so they formed a posse and went to find out."

R.D. sipped coffee again. "When I was a youngster

several old timers were still alive and told me it was a sight that could make a man go mad. That old abbey has surely seen its share of ghoulish activity."

Deedra felt a shiver of fear. "Then the abbey remained empty until the Embusteros moved in?"

"No. It was temporarily used during World War II to house recovering wounded military people."

"Anything mysterious go on during that time?"

R.D. grinned. "I knew you would ask that. I can't say for sure, but it was at that time that the wounded men there started referring to the place as that 'awful abbey.' The name stuck, and very few remember that it is really Anthea Abbey."

"Hm," Deedra muttered. Her mind conjured up the malefic old abbey. It certainly did have a lurid history and that made the tales of strange happenings believable to most of the townspeople.

"Have you reported Curt Ralston's disappearance to the media yet?" she asked.

"Not yet. I was asked not to. The F.B.I. wanted to work as quietly and carefully as possible. But of course, now that the whole town knows about it, I'm going to have to print the story. Mrs. Ralston is under Dr. Harris' care at the hospital and everyone who can is out looking for Curt Ralston."

"Where does Sandy Harris live?"

"In a huge house near the ravine, overlooking the lake. You can't miss it, just take Lake Drive and go all the way around to the end of the road. They call it Land's End, and it's a good name for it since the property just drops off into that deep arroyo. Dr. Harris had to put up an electric fence across the edge to keep the rattlesnakes out and to keep people from wandering too close to the edge."

"How in the world would it keep the snakes out?"

"He placed the lower wire just about half an inch off the ground. The rattlers find it…ah…startling to say the least. They often buzz out in anger when they hit it."

Deedra phoned Clete Bailey from the newspaper office. "The delivery boy who found Sharlee's note is missing. Sure you didn't know that when you sent me up here?"

"What? Give!" Clete took the information for the late edition.

After telling Clete everything she had learned she said, "I'm now going over to talk to Sandy Harris who was Sharlee's closest friend. Then, about dusk, I'm going back out to the abbey and prowl around."

"Deedra, do you think that's wise? There has to be something sinister going on there! Those rumors obviously have some kind of basis in fact. You shouldn't go out there alone!"

"Clete, just remember that you sent me up here to get a story on Sharlee Devon. The only way I'm

going to do that is to find out what's going on up at
the abbey. Now, if you've changed your mind about
that story, then I'll just relax and wait to see what
happens about the missing delivery boy."

"All right," Clete answered in a glum tone as if he
regretted sending her there.

Following R.D.'s directions, she had no trouble locating the Harris' home. Stately houses, tall trees and
bright lawns surrounded them. Most of the houses on
that street were traditional two-story, though several
were of Victorian architecture.

The Harris home was a combination of English
Tudor and modern Victorian. She could see a range
of jagged mountains beyond the wide ravine behind
the house, giving the house the appearance of standing on a low cloud. The ravine was almost straight
down. A gazebo graced the side lawn near a cluster
of acacia trees. A waterfall had been cleverly placed
to camouflage the huge boulders that had proved too
heavy to move.

The sound of light footsteps running downstairs
was in answer to the bell summons. The door was
opened by one of the most beautiful women Deedra
had ever laid eyes on. She was tall and willowy with
exotic, slanting green eyes and black brows that ac-
centuated their sensuous mien. The color on her lips
only emphasized her creamy complexion so free of
wrinkles that Deedra felt instant envy. Her hair was

dark and luxuriant. Sandy Harris lived up to all those shampoo ads that had featured her in the previous decade.

"Yes?"

Deedra introduced herself. "I need some information and I think you can help me."

Sandy Harris gave her an inquisitive stare. It was a probing look from someone who, in the past, had been interviewed by the famous of the media. She was suddenly warily alert.

She ushered Deedra into a spacious hall. At the far end of it, a curving stairwell rose toward an elegant balcony. Scrolled pillars supported a Doric archway leading to a large living room. The room was light and airy with wide windows that overlooked the lake, the front lawn and the flower gardens. The view of the lake was probably unsurpassed. The water was a clear blue, and there was a boat dock just across the road. Several boats were on the lake, but she didn't see any water-skiers or jet skis.

"No jet skiers?" she asked.

"No, they aren't allowed on the lake. It makes it bad for fishing and they bring the wrong kind of crowd here. This is a place for fishermen, swimmers and sail boaters. The rule keeps things calm around the lake." She paused. "Tell me what it is you would like to know."

"I'll level with you. I'm doing a story on Sharlee

Devon, and have been informed that you two were close friends. I need a clue to her sudden reclusiveness."

Sandy gestured in a helpless sort of way. "I haven't a clue. One day we were making plans to get back into modeling or movies, the next day Ricardo was refusing to let me see her. That's it. That's all I know. Sharlee never got in touch with me after that even though I sent her letters and tried to make contact by phone."

"Do you think she is mentally ill like Ricardo claims?"

"I can't believe that! She was fine the day before," Sandy replied.

"What do you really think?" Deedra challenged.

Sandy gave her a long, speculative look.

"I think Ricardo is keeping her captive. If anyone is mad, I think its Ricardo. From the few encounters I've had with him since Sharlee and I stopped talking, he doesn't even appear to be the friendly Ricardo I met earlier and was acquainted with. This…ah…man seems altered, as if overnight he's had a character change. There is something different about him. A slight change in appearance, a definite change in actions, and he appears to have aged."

The hair on the nape of Deedra's neck suddenly tingled. "What do you mean by that?"

"I can't say exactly. It's as if he is a multiple

personality. He seems to have grown older and sterner, lost his friendly smile. Does insanity do that to a person?"

Deedra was silent a moment before suggesting, "I'm not sure. Do you think he could be an impostor?"

"I've thought of that, but how could anyone look like Ricardo, talk like him and have the same tall frame?"

Deedra nodded. "Perhaps he was playing a role earlier and when they moved into the abbey he reverted to his real self. He was in a place where he could control Sharlee. There are rumors of strange things that happen in and around the abbey. What have you heard?"

"That there's a huge boy running about, that he has often scared teenagers away from an area famous for necking. That some of the young people have seen a ghost-like figure roaming about on the grounds, and that if they try to cross the bridge, lights go on in the abbey. Things like that, but there weren't any rumors until after they moved into that ghoulish old abbey. Really, I couldn't understand them even purchasing that old mausoleum! Ricardo claimed it was perfect for his experiments; that noises and unexpected lights wouldn't bother neighbors since they wouldn't have any. And he was always worried that someone was going to steal his inventions. My husband, David, says many inventors are paranoid like that. I must say that

David didn't find it strange that Ricardo would want a big old place like that."

"Did you hear that the missing Ralston boy found a note that Sharlee had thrown out the window?"

"Yes."

"Do you think his disappearance has anything to do with Sharlee's plight?"

"I thought of that, but what purpose would it serve? It would only focus attention on Ricardo and Sharlee and that's not what Ricardo wants right now."

Deedra nodded, but it was not in agreement. "I have another note Sharlee threw out the window for me." She handed the note to Sandy.

"This means Sharlee's had a baby! Did she give any indication about how old the child is?" There were tears in Sandy's eyes.

"No. R.D. says no one has been allowed to visit up there. Now, either the child is Ricardo's or one of the ghosts that are reported to haunt that place. Sharlee and the child are in dire danger. Anything you can tell me might help. Ricardo keeps Sharlee under constant closed circuit surveillance. I actually saw her on a monitor."

Sandy's eyes brimmed over and tears ran down her suddenly pale face.

FIVE

"You're certain you don't know how old the child is?" Sandy asked again.

"No. I need you to confide in me, Sandy. If I'm to help Sharlee, I have to know everything you know. She looks awful, like a ghost, has a haunted helpless look and she is very thin, actually frail. I don't know how long she would be able to live under those conditions."

Sandy gave her a probing stare, a look that was meant to find any duplicity.

"You have to swear that you won't print a word of it. I won't tell you anything unless you promise. And, anyway, I can't prove a word of what I have to say."

Deedra promised.

Sandy continued. "Sharlee and I went to the city several times where we met with contacts in the movie business and some modeling agents. People we already knew. Sharlee told me she was in love with a young movie producer who was just getting started and needed financial backing. It was only a little while, perhaps two or three weeks later, that Ricardo ordered me off his property. I don't know if

Sharlee has seen or heard from the young man since. He hasn't contacted me about her anyway."

"What's this producer's name?"

Sandy hesitated. "I don't want to get him into trouble, Deedra."

Deedra nodded. "I understand that, I also understand that someone has to help Sharlee."

Sandy studied her brightly polished fingernails and then sighed. "His name is Trent Kettering, and he isn't well-known yet."

Deedra had never heard of him, and wondered if Sharlee had lied about his real name.

"Have you ever been inside the awful abbey?"

Sandy nodded. "When they were doing the remodeling. I often went through it with Sharlee."

"Can you draw a sketch of the floor plan? I only got to see the hall and Ricardo's lab."

Sandy was obviously surprised by Deedra's request, though immediately went to a desk and extracted paper and pencils.

"You actually toured the old turret?"

Sandy shivered. "Yes. It's an awfully scary, gloomy place. Even then it was reported haunted, you know."

"Just who is supposed to haunt it?" Deedra watched as Sandy sketched out the floor plans.

"I don't know, I never asked."

"Was Sharlee frightened about living there?"

"Yes, she seemed very upset in the turret part. I was really shocked when I learned that she spends most of her time there now."

"Who told you that?"

Sandy shrugged. "That's the gossip. My husband, David, has even heard about it. Since then he's been very curious about Sharlee, and asks questions about her. I understand that he suggested to Ricardo that Sharlee would benefit from a medical check-up. Ricardo told him to mind his own business."

"Then your husband isn't aware that there's a baby up at the abbey?"

"He's never even hinted at it!" Sandy's eyes were wide with surprise.

"Then he isn't the doctor that Ricardo says he consulted about Sharlee's mental condition?"

Again Sandy showed surprise. "No, of course not. He isn't a psychiatrist or psychologist."

"Is he curious about why Sharlee shut you out of her life?"

"Yes, of course. But he seems to have accepted Ricardo's explanation." A glum expression crossed Sandy's face. "I used to think if I disguised myself I might get past Ricardo, then realized he would instantly see through it. It would only have made things more difficult for Sharlee."

"Did you ever go to the sheriff?"

"Yes." Sandy returned to the sketch. "The sheriff

went out there, and Ricardo gave him that 'my wife's in a fragile mental state' routine. Since then David just won't discuss it."

Deedra lapsed into silence, watching Sandy finish the sketch. The floor plan was like a maze.

"Remember to get in touch with me if you recall anything that might be useful in helping Sharlee. Just the fact that Ricardo monitors her on that damned surveillance circuit is monstrous, dehumanizing."

Again tears filled Sandy's eyes. She handed the sketch to Deedra. It was more detailed than Deedra had expected.

"Sandy, I hope you won't tell anyone my real reason for being here in Bermondy. It's better for everyone if they don't realize that I'm an investigative reporter."

"I don't think anyone would find it strange with Curt Ralston missing," Sandy replied.

Deedra sighed. It was true that a missing child attracted the media as nothing else did. She wanted to question Sandy about Curt Ralston but decided that it was the law's business. Sandy's husband might resent her questions since he was keeping the boy's mother under sedation in the hospital. She had learned all she could from Sandy Harris.

Sandy led her up the hall. "You'll let me know if you hear anything about Sharlee?"

"Yes."

"I have the awful feeling that it's already too late to help her!" Sandy sniffled.

"Let's hope you're wrong about that!"

Outside, Deedra glanced toward the ravine.

"Do you mind?" She walked toward the edge of the deep arroyo, noting the electric fence R.D. had described a few feet beyond the green lawn. "The land really does drop off back here!"

Sandy Harris gave her a rueful smile. "Yes. I keep hoping that Curt Ralston didn't fall into that ravine. Even if the fall didn't kill him, the rattlesnakes might."

Deedra shuddered. Snakes were her anathema.

FROM THE NEWSPAPER OFFICE she called Clete Bailey again. Keeping her voice low she said, "Find out all you can about a movie producer named Trent Kettering. Get Deke Thomas to talk to him and try to find out about his relationship with Sharlee…and have Deke get in touch with our sheriff friends. We need someone I can trust absolutely. This man…ah…has put his wife under constant surveillance. It's sadistic! As a woman I am furious! She's at his mercy twenty-four hours a day!"

Clete chose to ignore her remarks.

"That missing boy been located yet?"

"No. It's my guess that Curt got curious about Sharlee after finding that note and decided to see what he could do about helping her. I think Curt was caught on the grounds perhaps by old Hannah. That place has basements and sub-cellars. And Hannah was carrying a shovel as if she had just used it to bury something."

"My God, Deedra. You make the place sound like some medieval bastion where they put people in chains underneath in dark labyrinths," Clete challenged.

"That's about what it is. Sandy Harris is convinced of it. Just impress on Deke that it's quite a dangerous assignment."

"Right."

Deedra rang off and called the NBC affiliate station in the nearby metropolis. She asked for Chuck Preston. Fortunately he was in his office and answered immediately.

"Deedra Masefield here. I'm up in Bermondy. Can you guess why?"

"Sharlee Devon?"

"Yes. Can you give me a run down on your visit there?"

"You mean at the Awful Abbey? How important is this, Deedra?"

"Sharlee's in danger. A newspaper delivery boy who found a note Sharlee threw out the window is missing. The F.B.I. is here. Sharlee has a baby, and old Ricardo won't allow her to even go outside. He monitors her on a surveillance system."

"Do you think Ricardo is responsible for the boy's disappearance?"

"I have a hunch that he is."

Chuck Preston swore. "I can't tell you this over the phone, don't have the time anyway. Can you meet me at Point Triesta in the morning? I'm due near there to interview someone. An anonymous informer."

"Yep. Where and what time?"

"I should be there by eight. There's a restaurant near the wharf at the north end of town. The Tidewater. I'll meet you there."

"Right." She found R.D. staring at her when she hung up.

"You don't let any grass grow under your feet, do you?"

"No time for dilly-dally, R.D. Investigative reporters have to get there first to get the facts, and the scoop. Let me see your files on the banker, the doctor, and Ricardo again. I especially want to look at a photo of Ricardo."

With a gleam in his eyes, R.D. started toward the basement to fill her request.

Kortney Vickers entered, jauntily swinging her handbag. She gave R.D. a sweet smile, a smile Deedra interpreted as a sign of love. R.D. continued on his way to the basement for the files without appearing to notice Kortney's smile.

Kortney was definitely surprised to find her there,

and after a greeting, settled behind her desk. Deedra felt Kortney's covert scrutiny from time to time.

In David Harris' file she found articles on his sensational house named Land's End. She found stories about his marriage to Sandy, who at the time was a famous model for a popular shampoo manufacturer. There was no hint of scandal.

Calvin Ralston, the banker, had received a loan from Reuben Zolar, the casino owner, to open his bank. Had he angered the gamblers up at Zolar's mountain retreat? Had they kidnapped the boy in retaliation? Did the citizens of Bermondy realize the insidious influence Zolar might have on their town? It was a quiet town to be sure, and so far free of youth gang activity. Yet what about the money that supported the business enterprises? There was no real industry in Bermondy, what did the residents do to earn their living?

Ricardo's file showed a photo of him and his young wife, the famous Sharlee Devon. At that time there had only been a hint of the streaked hair and Ricardo's smile looked quite friendly. The man in this photo seemed quite different from the man who had taken Deedra on a tour through his laboratory. A subtle, malevolent look had changed Ricardo's features.

The article listed Ricardo's inventions and mentioned his four previous wives. Three of the women had died and left him scads of money or large insurance benefits. One of the dead wives had been the heiress to a chain-store fortune. She had died of pneumonia in their home. Strange. Why hadn't the woman been in a hospital? It couldn't have been lack of finances. There had been an autopsy, lab tests proving the presence of pneumonia. There was a note stating that the D.A. had said, "No, I don't think the doctor expected her to die." This left a suspicion that lingered in the minds of several news people, but the public had accepted it…and conveniently forgotten it.

Ricardo was worth several million dollars. There were always IRS inquiries. There were complaints made about the noises he made during his inventing processes. But Ricardo was a devious man and had learned to hide his money. Sharlee had been a millionaire when she married Ricardo, and now he controlled her money and resources as well. What about that money? Where was it, if there was anything left of it?

Was Sharlee Devon destined to rest among Ricardo Embustero's buried wives?

SIX

THEY DISCUSSED the possibility that Ricardo had murdered his heiress wife.

"He could have," Deedra reminded, "by placing a pillow over her face until she smothered. Back then they didn't have the forensic capabilities they do now. It wouldn't have changed the autopsy report unless the pathologist used extremely modern techniques."

"Does," R.D. challenged, "that make you think he is trying to kill Sharlee?"

"I think," she sighed, "that he is trying to infer that she's mentally unstable, perhaps so he can get control of her money. It would drive most people bananas to be watched on that surveillance thing all day, and that's probably part of his plan. And it keeps her from escaping."

"What a creep!" Kortney exclaimed.

They had forgotten Kortney could overhear and quickly became quiet. Whispering, R.D. said, "You think it's a case of inventor gone mad?"

"No, I think it's a case of a husband gone killer. If he's murdered the other women, then he's probably waiting for a chance to do Sharlee in. He's only divorced one of them. He can't take chances, though, with people inquiring about Sharlee all the time. He just has to wait until he's established the fact that she might 'harm herself.' The longer he keeps her captive there, the more her physical and emotional state is going to deteriorate. Then if she should suddenly throw herself down the stairs or out the window, or even cut her wrists, well, Ricardo tried to prevent that, didn't he?"

"Oh, yeah!" R.D. breathed in sudden shock. "That kind of monitoring and mind control is known to be dangerous. I read that it has turned many military people into living robots. They just respond to whatever is commanded of them. Ricardo could plant the idea in Sharlee's mind that her only way of escaping is to kill herself."

"Except for one thing," Deedra reminded, "Sharlee has a baby now. She isn't going to abandon that child. She especially isn't going to let Ricardo have him if she has any life left at all. That may be why he hasn't been able to accomplish that final act yet. It must be hell for her up there!"

Deedra glanced toward Kortney and found her busy with a customer. "It's not generally known, but there's a process called subliminal control, something like that. The subliminal images are flashed across the TV screen so rapidly they can't be seen by the naked eye, but the mind perceives them. In this way they can control the mind's thoughts or plant ideas into the victim's thoughts. It is such an outrageous concept that the government finally created a law against it. Who knows what a madman or one determined to get control of his wife's money could do with such an idea?" Deedra said quickly.

R.D. scratched his head; his eyes were dark with speculation. "I do remember reading something about that," he said quietly.

"It raised quite a ruckus back in the '1960s," Deedra sighed. "However, that's not solving the problem here. How do we get Sharlee out of there?"

R.D. seemed to be out of ideas. Every inducement he had tried before Deedra arrived had been unsuccessful.

"I'm going up to the abbey after a while. I'm hoping that Ricardo doesn't have the grounds monitored. I'm sure the gates and driveways probably are."

She shook her head when R.D. started to object. "Where can I get a decent meal around here?" she interjected, cutting him off.

R.D. directed her to the Deep Canyon Cafe up the street.

Walking there was a pleasant interlude. The town had a relaxed atmosphere that hadn't yet been disturbed by Curt Ralston's disappearance. Which was, she sighed, only a matter of hours away. When the media arrived with their TV cameras the town would be in turmoil. The town's streets and businesses had graphic names derived from the gold discoveries in the mid-1800's. There were plentiful tales of fabulous wealth gathered by early prospectors who came here and other points west in search of King Gold. It had been a fabulous time that had given California its mystique and added to the tales of San Francisco's "gold coast." The people she passed smiled in a friendly way and Deedra felt a friendly rapport there.

The restaurant was very clean. The food was served the way truck drivers like it: hot and plenty of it. She sat near a window watching the people and lingering over the excellent coffee.

The F.B.I. men entered and took a booth at the far end, out of Deedra's eavesdropping. She wondered if the Ralstons had received a ransom note yet, and what the lawmen had concluded about Curt's disappearance. In the city, Deedra would have introduced herself and questioned them. Now she merely wanted to go unrecognized, not cause any ripples. She had been ordered to stay away from cases the F.B.I. was in charge of before, they had interceded, and she had been unable to earn her front-page story. She hoped the man who thought he recognized her wouldn't remember who she was or where he had seen her.

Over a second cup of coffee, she studied Sandy's

sketch of the abbey's floor plans. She had to know how to get out of that place should the need arise. She noted that if Sharlee was in the turret rooms, she couldn't enter the area above Ricardo's lab unless she went down the stairs, then up the stairs on the east side near the front door. The house faced south. The ravine ran north behind the house and alongside the grounds on the west side. That ravine prevented entrance to the grounds from the west. It appeared the only way to get onto the grounds was by way of the road and across the old bridge. To the south and just across the road from the abbey was a thick wooded area. After considering it carefully, she decided that the only way to get Sharlee away was to go out through the front door and use the shelter of the foliage along the drive. She could scurry through the gate and go across the road into the thick woods. The problem with that was that Ricardo probably had the front gates under his surveillance system. They would just have to deal with that challenge when and if it arrived.

When she returned to the newspaper office, the F.B.I. men's battered old car was parked in front of the bank again.

She greeted R.D. with, "F.B.I. at the bank again."

He went to the window and peered through the slats, finally turning back to Deedra with a frown.

"No ransom note yet?" she asked.

"No," R.D. sighed. "Do you suppose the F.B.I. are setting a trap? It's obvious that everyone in town now knows that Curt is missing, and has probably guessed that they are federal men. If the F.B.I. men are waiting for a ransom note, why didn't they park that wreck of a car on a side street where it wouldn't attract such attention and go into the bank separately?"

Kortney listened to them in silence. If she had any thoughts about the situation she kept them to herself.

"I'm sure they know what they're doing, R.D." She placed the sketch Sandy had drawn on the desk. "Sandy drew the floor plans for me."

R.D. looked over her shoulder.

Deedra tried to memorize the location of the rooms. It was no easy task since the rooms were often interconnected; obviously a design holdover from the cell-like rooms occupied by the nuns. "There's only that main hallway which is divided halfway down by a heavy stairwell leading to rooms on the second floor. Just inside the front door are two sets of stairs. The left one leads to the turret, the other to rooms on the second and third floors above Ricardo's laboratory. There is only one set of stairs leading to each floor and no way of getting from the turret to other parts of the house without going down to the ground floor. There is, however, a narrow stairway from the turret to the tower located just above it, but no way of escaping from the tower."

Deedra shook her head. "I had hoped there was an outside stairway, a way of getting down from the tower room." She leaned back in the chair. "Sandy must have spent a lot of time at the abbey to have been able to draw this sketch."

"Yeah. I can't believe there is only one set of stairs to each floor."

"You know how it was with a cloister. They didn't want the nuns 'socializing' at night. By making it difficult to reach other floors they deterred visiting."

"How awful," Kortney muttered.

Deedra phoned Clete Bailey. "Did you tell Deke Thomas what I wanted him to do?"

"Yes. He's out talking to that movie producer now. Don't be surprised if he shows up there. He appeared worried about you and the news of the boy's disappearance gives him a perfect excuse to go to Bermondy."

"Deke isn't going to let me get an exclusive on this story?"

"You need help getting Sharlee out of there, don't you?" Clete challenged.

"Right." She replaced the receiver in both an excited and disappointed mood. She was in love with Deke Thomas who worked for the same newspaper. But Deke avoided marriage as if it was some strange disease he dared not catch. Deedra wanted children, and her biological clock was ticking away. It had been several months since she and Deke had even discussed marriage. In the meantime she had decided not to wait around for Deke and had started dating other men. They typically lacked the chemistry vibes Deke managed to set off in her. As a news reporter she was disappointed now, wanting to get an exclusive, but knowing she would probably need help.

Deedra Masefield and Deke Thomas had been a team ever since she had gone to work for the *Daily Spokesman*. Though she had solved several murders, Deke had often been there to help. They had shared intimate moments and she knew that no one could ever really replace Deke in her life. But Deke didn't want to be a permanent fixture in her environment so she was forced to think of other alternatives. She wasn't going to miss motherhood just because of Deke's reluctance to commit. She would find someone else to raise a family with, someone not afraid of commitment.

She ran her hands through her short curls and sighed.

The sigh caused R.D. to question her. "What's wrong?"

"Nothing, really. Just thinking that life gets complicated even when you don't want it to."

"That's for sure!" Kortney spouted and glanced at R.D.

R.D. blushed and turned away, causing Deedra to wonder once again what there was between them. R.D. wasn't married so that couldn't be a complication.

Dusk was only a few minutes away when Deedra, armed with a flashlight and a snub-nosed revolver, drove out to the old abbey. The way seemed dismal with shadows creeping across the road. A heavy mist gathered in the clusters of thick growth and hovered along the ground in silent glens. It was a scary drive, enough to start her imagination conjuring up all sorts of spooky things. Right then if anyone had told her the abbey was really haunted, she would have sincerely believed it. She wondered at Curt Ralston's courage in riding his bicycle along that lonely road. In late fall or winter there must have been fog and cold winds here. Had what happened to Curt happened right there on that desolate road?

She rounded a sharp curve and was suddenly at the narrow bridge spanning the ravine. Not wanting to attract Ricardo's attention, she turned the car around and parked it in a wide space just off the road.

Placing car keys in the hip pocket of her jeans and the gun and flashlight in her jacket pockets, she dropped on all fours and crawled across the bridge. Ricardo, she reckoned, might have the bridge monitored but she hoped he wouldn't place the sensors so low that they would detect every dog or wild animal crossing the bridge.

Once across, she rushed into the shadow of an old oak and waited. If her presence had been detected there would certainly be some kind of reaction. Nothing happened.

She scurried from tree to shrub and crawled through the front gates. She finally reached the east side of the house. Ricardo's lab was located there but heavy draperies prevented any light from filtering through. Before doing any real prowling, she wanted to know where both Ricardo and Hannah were.

She crept around the abbey going toward the back. That side of the abbey lacked the foliage that permeated the rest of the grounds. There were no shrubs and only a few trees. She stood in the shadow of an old tree, studying her surroundings. The back yard was bleak. No attempt had been made to camouflage the deep ravine, though a few boulders rested along the edge.

Suddenly she heard the back door creak open and caught a glimpse of Hannah's voluminous black dress.

Deedra stepped into deeper shadow.

Hannah walked to the edge of the ravine and glanced around both sides of the house as if she suspected someone's presence. She strode to the west side, then back toward the east, walking very close to Deedra's hiding place.

Deedra saw her shake her head. Then Hannah halted and stood quite still as if listening. She shook her head again, and glanced around. Had darkness not been closing in, Hannah would probably have walked out toward the front gates. Instead, she snuffled like a dog trying to pick up the scent of another presence, shook her head again and stomped along with her voluminous dress in full sail.

Deedra heard the back door slam shut.

SEVEN

A WIND SPRANG UP and whistled over the ravine, whining in the crooks and crannies around the old abbey. The old trees bent and swayed in shadowy gyrations.

Since Hannah had moved freely about the back yard, she thought the maybe it wasn't being monitored on Ricardo's surveillance system.

She crept around the house, finally reaching a place where she could see through the window next to the back door. It was a porch with the kitchen just beyond. Hannah moved in and out of her vision. Deedra was happy to determine Hannah's whereabouts and reckoned that she would remain in the kitchen area until supper preparations and the meal were over.

Deedra crept around to the west side where the shadows were thick and deep, and definitely scary. She had a dread of snakes, for her they were panic-producers, and spiders were a close second. Her heart hammered and her mouth felt dry. She wanted to cough and hoped that Ricardo was unaware of her presence. A noise sent her skulking into the thick foliage where she waited and watched.

Nothing moved. No sounds echoed among the heavy vines. She quietly crept to the rock wall that divided the property from the ravine arriving just as she heard the back door creak open. Someone swinging a flashlight went along the worn path toward the ravine. She glimpsed the shadow of Hannah's flowing dress.

Keeping close to the rock wall, she scurried toward the ravine, intent on finding out what Hannah was doing. The flash beam vanished. She thought Hannah was off to her right somewhere.

Deedra was unable to see Hannah. She dropped to the ground and hugged her knees. She was suddenly very, very afraid. Behind Deedra was the ravine and ahead in the dark shadows was Hannah. What if Hannah caught her there? Would she take her to Ricardo or just push her into the ravine? It had, she reflected, been unwise to follow Hannah, but right now she had to cope with that mistake.

As she strained to hear sounds of Hannah's approach, she was suddenly alerted to the fact that the night birds had gone silent causing a strained hush, a heavy, somehow threatening silence.

A twig snapped a few feet in front of her.

Deedra smothered a scream.

Suddenly the back door screeched open and light spilled onto the steps, outlining Hannah's black clad figure directly in front of her.

"Hannah, where the hell are you? Get this supper on the table!"

She heard Hannah mutter something like a curse. Hannah then threw a heavy rock down, hitting Deedra on the shoulder.

Pain shot through Deedra's arm and her fingers started to tingle.

Hannah glanced around, the dress making a wide swathe, then headed for the house, her figure in dark silhouette against the light from the open door. The smell of Hannah's unwashed body lingered, causing Deedra a moment of nausea.

She waited until Hannah entered the house before moving. She took several deep breaths to ease the pain, to prevent the moans. She tried to steady the fear that swept through her.

The wind had increased to thrusting bursts that caused a groaning sound around the abbey. The wind noises covered the sound of her movements as she crept along the rock wall to the road. She dared not use her own flashlight.

The wall was covered with lichen and scaly things, and occasionally she had to brush spider webs aside. She shuddered at the sight of the webs. It took considerable time to reach the road. The night had deepened into that darkness just before the moon begins to traverse the heavens. When at last she reached the road, intuition told her to wait in the shadows, not to try and cross that old bridge just yet. Besides, her arm pained.

That imp of caution proved right on target. Hannah's black figure was silhouetted against the roadway as she marched toward the bridge.

Deedra moved into deeper shadow just beyond the wall and off of the Embustero property.

Hannah halted before stepping onto the bridge. She seemed to look about as if she expected to find someone there. Her whole body expressed suspicion and wariness. Deedra wouldn't have been surprised to see her tremble.

The moon had peeked over the horizon, outlining Hannah's tall black silhouette against the road and bridge railings. Hannah began fiddling with something on one of the railings and Deedra knew it was some kind of electronic gadget to detect visitors. How did they dare to put something on a public owned bridge?

She smothered a groan. Now, how was she going to get across the bridge without the Embusteros knowing she had been snooping around? She could get away, of course, but she didn't want to let them know of her spying, a thing that might make things more dangerous for Sharlee and her baby…a thing that might force Ricardo into desperate action.

As she watched, she began to wonder why Hannah

was so worried that someone might enter the property. Everyone knew that Sharlee was there; it had never been a secret. That meant there was something else they needed to keep hidden. It had to be something serious to place a surveillance gadget on a bridge that wasn't even on their property. They were obviously worried about something. Was that something Curt Ralston? Had the visit from the F.B.I. forced them to take special precautions?

Finally Hannah finished her task and strode by Deedra's hiding place with the long strides common to tall people. It occurred to Deedra that if anyone saw her now they could easily conclude that she was a nun-ghost. Her dark habit, the long bulky dress and just being outside at night would cause questions or inspire fear. Some of the rumors were starting to make sense.

Hannah halted at the driveway entrance and looked back toward the bridge. She was evidently studying the roadsides. Then, shrugging, she disappeared through the gates.

Deedra was still following her intuition and quietly waited in the shadows. Her precaution was rewarded.

Hannah reappeared, striding up the road toward the bridge where she halted almost directly in front of Deedra. It was as if some instinct told her that someone lurked there. Fortunately, she didn't seem to have a flashlight with her this time. But it was plain that Hannah suspected someone lingered near the bridge. At that moment Deedra realized that Hannah was more dangerous than Ricardo. What would Hannah have done if she had found Curt Ralston prowling about?

Fear grated across Deedra's nerves. If they found the boy alive she would be very surprised. A shudder shook her slim frame.

At last Hannah seemed to be somewhat satisfied there was no one there. She trudged off in her stiff-jointed way up to the driveway where she glanced about again, and disappeared.

Deedra, though she let out a long-held breath in a hiss, remained cautious and did not move. She waited for what seemed like an eon. She had to make certain that Hannah had returned to the house for good. When at last the night birds took up their twittering again, she scurried from her hiding place and went to the bridge.

Shielding the beam of her flashlight, she examined the electronic gadget Hannah had placed under the railing. It had been put into operation by using a key and Deedra didn't seem to be able to turn it off without that key.

Perspiration sprouted over her body and the wind chilled her. She stood there undecided. How could she cross over the ravine without tripping the sensor? The sensible thing to do was just boldly walk across.

Deedra glanced back toward the front entrance and walked into the woods that were across the road. She soon discovered that she couldn't reach her car from that direction because of the ravine. She glanced toward the abbey. A frail light shone from the turret windows, and there were faint lights illuminating the back of the old monstrosity, indicating that the Embusteros were still in the kitchen area. But even as she stood there watching, Hannah opened the front door and disappeared within.

Deedra caught her breath. Hannah had been outside and hadn't seen her. Perhaps she had been searching around the art studio and summerhouse.

A few moments after Hannah went inside, light shone through the front windows throwing faint beams across the front steps and lawn near the windows.

Deedra hurried back to the bridge where she aimed the flashlight under the bridge outlining its steel girders. Though the bridge was nearly a century old, it was sturdily built and appeared to have adequate handholds. She pointed the beam into the ravine below where the dark void caused her another shudder, but on the far side was a ledge atop a shallow slope only ten or fifteen feet below the bridge leading up to the far side. If she reached that slope, she would escape undetected.

After considering the options for a few moments she decided she could go hand over hand grasping the girders, then drop to the ground on the ledge with a minimum of injury. That would avoid setting off the motion sensor and perhaps a surveillance camera. It shouldn't be too difficult. She had often played for hours on the "monkey bars" at school, and knew she could hold her own weight. Actually, she reminded herself, she had developed an agility that was the envy of the more plump girls whose arm muscles couldn't sustain their weight.

For a moment she thought the hell with the Embusteros surveillance system. It was after all a public bridge. They didn't own it. But, she reminded herself, she wasn't the only one in danger here. Curt Ralston might still be alive and hidden in the cellars of the abbey, to say nothing about Sharlee's plight and that of her child who might be sacrificed as well. Deedra didn't want all that on her conscience.

Making certain the gun and flashlight were secure in her jacket pockets, she stooped and grasped a girder. She swung out over the ravine. The sudden pull on her shoulders, especially the injured one, was greater than she had anticipated. It was all she could do to hold on. Gritting her teeth, she began the hand over hand trek across the chasm, not daring to look down into its yawning void.

Pain shot through the shoulder injured by Hannah's

thrown rock. She tired rapidly and halfway over began to doubt she could reach the other side. Even her breathing became painful. The added weight and bulk of her jacket caused additional strain on her arm muscles. Waves of agony caused tremors, a trembling that made hanging onto the girders difficult. Where was Deke Thomas when she needed him? That thought brought her focus back on the task, this do or die thing, and gave her the determination not to end her life by dropping into that dark chasm where the rattlesnakes could get her.

After what seemed like a lifetime, she was only a few feet from the ledge. She centered her focus on placing one hand over the other and moving forward. She was always conscious of that dark void below her. Deedra didn't have the strength to lift her body onto the bridge or even hoist her body onto a girder. She just had to keep going though her breathing had become erratic, her heart sounds hammering in her ears.

Deedra's hand touched a scaly rope-like thing.

Her reaction was immediate. She heaved the snake into the night, quickly grasping the girder again.

The rattlesnake buzzed its anger from depths of the echoing ravine. Suddenly the night air was filled with the angry buzzing of snakes from that dark chasm below.

Shudders nearly caused her to let go, but the fact

that snakes were below and a resolution not to end up there gave her strength.

Perspiration ran anew and tears slid down her face. Please God, she prayed, if I must die don't let it be among those snakes! She dropped to the ground, unable to hang on any longer. Deedra was surprised to find she had landed on the very edge of the slope. Her fall caused a slight landslide that startled the rattlesnakes into buzzing anger again.

Groaning with terror, she scrambled to the top of the slope where she grasped a girder and climbed onto the road. Once away from the bridge she lay down and wept. After a long time of deep breathing, Deedra recalled that snakes liked to slither along roadsides after dark and this thought hurried her to the car, her flashlight guiding the way.

Deedra didn't even remember her drive back to Bermondy. She only recalled the sound of buzzing in her ears and the vision of that dark chasm in her mind's eye. But the pain in her arm and her sore shoulder muscles were a sharp reminder for the next few days. It only served to reinforce her fear of rattlesnakes. For a long while after that night, even other buzzing sounds could cause her a shudder.

Fog had settled in, and in several places it hovered over the road causing an added sense of isolation. Her whole body trembled and she only calmed when the lights of Bermondy came into view. Deedra realized that in the future, when she remembered Bermondy, it would be the welcoming lights she was seeing now that she would recall fondly, lights that suddenly released her from that terrifying grip of fear. The relief was immediate…and heady, causing her to feel quite giddy.

R.D. was anxiously awaiting her return. "Clete Bailey has been phoning every half hour. I was going to give you just fifteen more minutes, then start out after you."

"Just let me sit down, will you? Have you got a strong cup of coffee?"

R.D. noticed her nervousness and laced the coffee with something he kept in his desk drawer for emergencies. "What happened? Your face is all scratched, and your clothes are covered with dust."

"Any news of Curt Ralston yet?" She clutched the cup gratefully.

"No. There was a detective here looking for you. He wouldn't leave his name. Said he would check back later. Now give. What happened up at the abbey?"

She told him of her experience and of what she had learned from prowling about. She had to reassure R.D. that the snake had not bitten her.

"Do you think Curt is hidden at the abbey?" R.D. paced about anxiously.

"Hannah was certainly uneasy about something. She didn't see me, yet she was certainly alert as if she expected to catch someone prowling around. The visit from the F.B.I. might have caused her to be especially watchful. Perhaps she thought lawmen were posted about the grounds. She and Ricardo have something to hide, so they are certainly on guard. But her action in bugging the bridge is excessive and illegal. Most people wouldn't dream of going to that extreme, of actually installing an illegal device or a motion sensor on a bridge that wasn't even theirs! Hannah is definitely skittish about something."

"Yeah, and why was it Hannah and not Ricardo who searched about outside? The abbey is the only house or building around here that hasn't been searched. I'm certain Curt is up there somewhere. Hannah might have glimpsed him earlier and was out looking for him," R.D. remarked in a glum tone. "Oh, a guy by the name of Deke Thomas phoned, cussed something awful when he learned you had gone up to the abbey."

"Did he leave a message?"

"He said it was too involved to talk about on the phone."

"He didn't even hint at what he learned from that movie producer?"

"No."

Deedra sighed. "I'm going to drive over to Point Triesta. I'm supposed to meet Chuck Preston there at 8:00 in the morning. I think I'll sleep better tonight if

I'm away from deep canyons and thoughts of rattle-snakes. The ocean always has a calming effect on me."

Deedra drank another cup of coffee to fortify her for the long drive and bid R.D. goodnight.

Point Triesta was seventy-nine miles away, but the drive was not a scary one like the road leading to the abbey. Once she reached the ocean her old sense of self returned. Point Triesta was situated on jagged cliffs above the Pacific where giant waves crashed against solid rock, sometimes sending spray onto the cliff tops. There was no beach, for even at low tide the water was several feet deep at the base of the cliffs. The view, however, was unique. It was an awe-inspiring place where artists often gathered.

Deedra took deep breaths of the clean ocean air and allowed the sea breeze to riffle through her short curls. At that moment, the abbey seemed far away.

Deedra found found a restaurant where she ordered a hamburger, fries and a chocolate milk shake. Her misadventures had left her hungry and fast food was just the tonic she needed.

The motel next to the restaurant was still open and she was given the last cabin. It was moderately clean, reassuring her that she wouldn't discover crawly things on the walls and floor in the morning. The only irritating thing was the dark path leading to the cabin. These days, Deedra liked well-lighted places.

The ocean's lullaby put her to sleep within minutes. She awoke quite refreshed and ready to meet a new day's challenges. The experience of the previous day was muted, as if it had happened in a dream.

She phoned Clete from her cell phone before driving off to meet the famous news anchor. "You wouldn't believe the cruddy time I had getting across that old bridge without springing Hannah's electronic trap, Clete! I'll tell you about it sometime. Right now I want to find out what Deke has learned from that movie producer."

"Deke's on his way up there right now. He can tell you himself. The story about the missing boy hit every news media in the country this morning."

"Oh! Have the F.B.I. people anything to report?"

"Nope."

Chuck Preston was waiting for her at The Tidewater Restaurant. He had commandeered a table by a window that overlooked the ocean. The view was unsurpassed. Chuck gave her one of his famous smiles as she took the seat opposite him.

Deedra had to admit that Chuck was one of the most handsome men she had ever met. He possessed a carefree humor and dignity; his voice was resonant and memorable. She could see why his was a voice that captivated TV audiences.

"What's going on, Deedra? It must be important

for Clete to have sent you up there, especially after those Coleridge and Black murders."

She laughed. "You know Clete. He sends me out on whatever story he thinks is going to make front-page news. This is strange and scary, and I'm not sure you'll believe my adventures of last night. I'll tell you about them later. Right now I need to know about your visit to Anthea Abbey and how you got invited there. Just to let you know how important this is, Ricardo has Sharlee Devon under a surveillance system that is monitored 24 hours a day. She's absolutely terrified."

A frown like a dark cloud suddenly blotted out the smile on Chuck Preston's face.

"That really doesn't surprise me, Deedra. I tried to get Sharlee to leave with me but somehow Ricardo prevented it. I'm not sure just how he did it."

"Did Sharlee have a child then, or was she expecting one?"

"Hey, Deedra! I didn't have a thing going with Sharlee!"

"I didn't mean that," Deedra brushed the thought aside. "In a note she threw out near my car, she said she couldn't get the child away from Ricardo."

"Did she say whether it was her child or the missing Ralston boy? Sharlee did tell me she had something confidential to tell me. She never got a chance because Ricardo made certain we weren't left alone.

I thought it had something to do with the turret part of the house because she kept glancing that way and seemed to be listening for something. Every time I tried to talk to her, Ricardo would change the subject; kind of shut her up."

"You were there when?"

"About six months ago."

"The Ralston boy disappeared a week ago and he was the one who found the first note. In my note Sharlee stated she had a baby, which would mean an infant. Do you think it could be Ricardo's child?"

"I think it has to be. Ricardo wouldn't let anyone else within throwing distance of her."

"Why did you go to the abbey?" Deedra challenged.

"It wasn't a tryst with Sharlee, if that's what you mean. A movie mogul I know was really concerned about her, especially after he couldn't contact Sharlee personally. His studio notified the *L.A. Times,* and they got in touch with me. Between us, we decided that someone needed to go up there and really find out what was going on. Ricardo didn't want me to spend a weekend there—in fact he absolutely refused. So we got the manufacturer of one of his inventions to pressure Ricardo into it. They told him they needed the interview for the publicity, that his royalty checks would probably increase, and so on. Ricardo told them he would have to think it over. We all got the impression that he was either cleaning up a mess there or that he was instructing Sharlee about what she was to say and do. A few days later I was reluctantly invited to the abbey where I spent the most ghastly weekend of my life!"

Chuck shook his head in recollection, the remnants of fear reflected in his eyes.

EIGHT

"TELL ME!" Deedra had her elbows on the table, her hands cupping her face.

"I was all psyched up about the visit as you can imagine. It was a real scoop for me since no one else had ever been permitted to visit Sharlee there. Hollywood people were curious about her lifestyle, and, of course, the public was even more curious. Did you know there's an electronic eye at the front gates that lets Ricardo know when someone enters the property?"

Deedra nodded her head.

"That place is a maze of rooms that all lead back to the main front hall. A person needs painted lines on the floor to take you from one room to another. I thought it was damn gutsy for Ricardo to say that he had actually paid to have that place remodeled. It must have given the carpenters and those working there a helluva laugh. Though I don't know what it was like before the remodeling, it could have been a cluster of those cell-like rooms. Perhaps this is really an improvement.

"Anyway, he gave me a room on the second floor,

above his lab. If you know where the lab is located," when she nodded he continued, "in the far northeast corner overlooking that ravine. There was only one door and the only way to reach any other part of the house is to go to the stairs just off the main hall at the front of the house. There's a separate staircase to the third floor there and yet another staircase to the turret rooms. Each of those stairwells is divided by a partition on the landing so that the rooms on the west side are separated from those on the east side, even though they are on the same floor. Now wouldn't you think someone remodeling would change that?"

Chuck took a big gulp of coffee.

"It was very confusing, though of course, Sharlee might have adjusted to it after living there a while."

"I doubt that house has a calming effect on any-one's nerves," Deedra remarked.

"On the Friday night I arrived, I tried prowling about. That was after having been served dinner in the coldest dining room imaginable and by a woman with a Cyrano de Bergerac nose and a heavy cold. Her idea of having fun is probably capturing spiders." He sighed, and took another sip of coffee.

"Sharlee never said a word during that whole dinner. It was as if she was scared to death. She didn't even look at me the whole time even though I tried to include her in the conversation. I had met her several times earlier while she was making movies. It wasn't as if Sharlee didn't know who I was. Each time I tried to talk to her, Ricardo would head her off before she could reply and direct the conversation back to his inventions. He would actually remind me that my visit was primarily to learn more about his inventions. Ricardo flapped on and on about his genius, about how rotten his former wives were and how they had complained about the amount of time he had spent in his laboratory," Chuck looked at the table and shook his head, continuing, "and how they hadn't benefited when at last he became successful. Between Ricardo and that creepy long-nosed old woman with post-nasal drip, my appetite was not there. I shall never eat lamb stew again…if it was lamb stew."

Deedra started.

Chuck stared at her. "Yes, I honestly wondered what it was that we were eating. I have never tasted anything like it, and I hope I never do again."

Chuck took another sip of coffee, the look in his eyes reflecting something he couldn't quite put into words. "That night I was shooed off to bed like a naughty child at 8:00. Having nothing to do at twilight is very boring so I decided to do a little haunting myself. By that time I knew I wouldn't remain there until Sunday afternoon as had been arranged, so I had to take advantage of the time I was there. No sooner had I left my room that all sorts of scary things began to happen. Believe me, right away I really thought the old place was haunted! Every time I think of that weekend, I get cold chills." He paused as if reluctant to go on. "Well, I tried to get to the turret area where Sharlee was. I intended to talk to her, to find out what the hell was going on. But every time I tried to go there I ran into ghostly specters dancing along the hallways. I'm certain they were holographic images. Ricardo is quite capable in the trickery department, and I think the time he made us wait for the acceptance of my visit gave him time to set up those images. They would scare anyone, and if he uses them to keep Sharlee in her rooms at night, I can see why she hasn't made any attempt to escape."

"How does he create the images?"

Again Chuck sighed. "Pictures of non-existent objects can be created by interference with sound just as 3-D equipment is photographed. In other words, the sound is photographed, not the object. It acts like a mirage. You've seen how clear non-existent water is in a mirage. It's heat rising into the atmosphere. 3-D holographic tricks work the same way. You just see things that aren't really there."

Chuck took out a notebook and thumbed through it until he found a sketch. He showed it to Deedra. "I had to look this up after I got back to the TV station. I knew something about it when I was at the abbey, but I wasn't really sure about how the thing worked.

Ricardo is a very devious man, a dangerous man, and I think Sharlee is at risk."

"You never told anyone about this, Chuck?"

"Who would believe it, Deedra? They would think I spent the weekend in an alcoholic haze. I reported that Sharlee wasn't interested in making any more movies and that she appeared afraid and nervous. And that Ricardo was a hostile host. And that seemed to end the matter. I certainly never wanted to be reminded of it."

"You say that the images danced about, did they groan or anything like that?"

"No, they were just images. But I did catch a glimpse of a huge mutant walking around. He appeared to be a young boy grown to gigantic proportions. I only caught a glimpse of him as he disappeared into the kitchen. He had evidently been in the hall. Hannah shooed him into the kitchen with hissing, scolding words. I had the immediate and ugly thought that Ricardo had been doing some kind of experimentation on the boy and that the experiment had gone awry. But then I recalled that all his inventions were of the mechanical or electronic type." He paused a moment as if contemplating. "Since Hannah is such a grotesque example of a human being, I thought the mutant boy might be a relative of hers. There's also the chance that my glimpse of the mutant was just another of Ricardo's tricks. However, I really don't think so since he was with Hannah and she is real enough."

"That certainly explains the rumors of a monster up around the abbey," Deedra remarked. "R.D. Spenser thought it was just everyone's imagination. But then you are the only person I've met who admits seeing Hannah, and R.D. claims that he has never heard of her. R.D. actually thought I was hallucinating or making it up because he's lived here all this time and had never even heard of her existence. I'm glad you saw her several months ago which proves that she's been living at the abbey for the past couple of years."

"Sharlee is afraid of her," Chuck said. "She cringes every time Hannah gets near her."

"Do you really think she is Ricardo's sister?" Deedra challenged.

"I haven't the vaguest. She is tall like Ricardo and has dark eyes and hair. The resemblance ends there, however."

Deedra described her encounter with Hannah the night before and told him of her hellish trek crossing the bridge.

"God, Deedra, what does it feel like to touch a rattlesnake?"

"Scaly, cold, reptilian. A real shudder-maker."

Chuck shook his head, a wry grin tugged at the corners of his mouth.

"Take care, Deedra. Old Ricardo isn't going to let anyone poach on his preserves, and Sharlee is his preserve."

"Did Ricardo act the loving husband, seem to have anything but possessive control for Sharlee?"

Chuck shook his head. "Not that I could see. He just dominated the conversation, dominated what Sharlee did. And even dominated old Hannah."

"What do you make of all this, Chuck? Off the record. I know you've explained about the dancing ghosts. But that only explains Ricardo's attempt to make you believe that Sharlee is also seeing things, that it's causing her mental problems."

"Don't laugh, Deedra," Chuck frowned.

"Do I sound like I'm laughing? Just remember Curt Ralston is missing and he could be held captive at the abbey. And Sharlee is at least in emotional danger if not physical danger. Last night I went through an experience I would never care to repeat."

Chuck leaned back in his chair in a weary way that indicated his reluctance in confiding what he really thought. "I think Ricardo got a hold of a male child he wanted to experiment on and it resulted in the mutant I saw there. I think that's why Ricardo never really wants anyone to visit, and I think it is part of the reason that he doesn't allow Sharlee to leave. She would certainly tell people about the happenings there. And I'm afraid that Ricardo may have kidnapped the Ralston boy."

Deedra stared at him a moment. "In other words, you're telling me that you think Ricardo is a monster."

"Yes, Deedra, I'm certain that Ricardo Embustero is a monster."

NINE

RELUCTANTLY, DEEDRA drove back to Bermondy.
The day was oppressively hot and she hated to leave
the coastal breezes and the sight and sound of the
ocean. The nearly eighty mile drive loomed ahead
of her where none of those cooling breezes could
filter between the deep canyons and jagged mountain-
ous areas. After leaving the main highway she drove
through a long stretch where there were few houses
and no towns. That was until she reached the junction
with the highway where the Bermondy River rushed
alongside the road. By the time she reached the lake
on the outskirts of Bermondy, she was hot and cranky,
the car's air conditioner the only thing preventing her
from bursting into a fit of bad temper.

Chuck Preston's advice kept going through her
head. "Give up the idea, Deedra. Just drop it. No
one is ever going to prevail over old Ricardo. He's
within a husband's right to protect Sharlee from public
scrutiny. Especially if she really is in delicate health,
as Ricardo claims, and has been perceived by everyone who has seen her lately. Sharlee isn't at all like
her former self. She's lost that spark that attracted

the movie audience. Without a warrant to search the abbey and its cellars, and especially the turret rooms where Sharlee spends most of her time, there's nothing anyone can do. The only chance to search there is for Curt Ralston. If someone actually saw him on the abbey grounds just before he disappeared, Curt's finding that note might only be incidental. Sharlee might have thrown it out for anyone to find because the abbey may have had other visitors, how do we know?" Here Chuck had taken a deep breath.

"And if you keep prowling around it's only going to put Sharlee at greater risk. Just let it go, Deedra. The F.B.I. is in charge of Curt's disappearance, and that fact has put the Embusteros on guard. Even if a warrant could be obtained now, Ricardo and Hannah have had adequate warning and will have destroyed any evidence that the Ralston boy had ever been there. Most likely Hannah will now keep the mutant confined to the cellars most of the time. A glimpse of him might cause an investigation by human rights people or some other agency. But you can bet Ricardo and Hannah will not let anyone in or near the abbey if they can possibly keep them out."

Chuck had paused at that moment before adding, "It wouldn't surprise me if Ricardo suddenly allows Sharlee to answer a few phone calls. With him right there to censor her conversation, of course. Ricardo will find some way to soothe over any type of investigation. He's a very clever and devious man, and perhaps he has a lot of skeletons in those dank cellars. Just let it go, Deedra, before something happens to you!"

When she arrived at the newspaper, R.D. and the F.B.I. men were talking in low voices near a bank of file cabinets and Kortney was talking to someone on the phone.

She took a big city newspaper from the counter and began to read the story on the missing Curt Ralston. Deedra was so intent on the article about the boy that she didn't hear the tall, lean and handsome blond man stride up beside her.

"Hi!" he whispered in her ear.

"Deke! You scared me."

"Are we still nervous about skulking about in dark places at night, and picking up rattlesnakes?" he grinned. The redeeming thing about Deke was his enchanting smile. It was a smile that made most women want to smile back, the un-redeeming feature was that Deke took advantage of those females.

"It wouldn't have been nearly so frightening if you had been there to pick it up for me!" she retorted. "I see you are here with your camera and everything. Hoping to get a better picture of Sharlee?"

Deke looked pained. She suddenly recalled that Deke and Sharlee had once been an item. She felt contrite.

"Clete tells me that Daryl Walters chased you out of town again," he jabbed in retaliation.

"Not funny, Deke. Daryl is very serious about his intentions and he just never gives up. He has the impression that he can get me to marry him if he just hangs around long enough…or if you just disappear. Since no one else seems interested in marrying me he thinks all he has to do is just keep up the pursuit."

This had the desired effect on Deke Thomas. He quickly changed the subject to that of the missing Curt Ralston. "I hear there's no new clues, no ransom note."

Deedra nodded. "What did you learn from Trent Kettering, that young movie director?" she asked.

"I'll have to tell you later. Why don't we ride out to the abbey?"

"I have to contact the detective Gavin Blair sent first."

"Is that him?" Deke nodded to a man strolling along the sidewalk across the street. "He seems to like that stretch of sidewalk, he's walked up and down it several times now and he keeps glancing at his watch as if he's waiting for someone."

Deedra gave the man an appraising glance and headed out the door.

The man noticed them, nodded slightly and walked toward the end of the block where he crossed to their side of the street. They walked up the street to meet him.

He was a surprise to Deedra who actually didn't know what to expect. The man was a nondescript person who could easily get lost in a crowd. Deedra wasn't certain that if she saw him again she would even recognize him.

"Are you Gavin Blair's friend?" Deedra inquired.

"Yep. You must be Deedra Masefield. And I'll bet this is your sidekick, Deke Thomas."

Deke was taken aback by the recognition, and a little miffed at the term "sidekick." Being a man, he wanted to have Deedra termed his sidekick, wanted to be the one in charge. Deke answered in a flat tone, "Yep."

"Let's go for a ride." Deedra saw R.D. and the F.B.I. men standing on the sidewalk. No doubt R.D. was filling them in on who she and Deke were and she had no desire to be questioned by the federal men at that moment. Deedra led them to her car.

The detective had not yet told them his name and he didn't even after they were in the car and heading toward the abbey.

Finally the man said, "Just call me Nick. I don't give a last name when I'm working on a case like this. Protects me, protects you. I understand that the *Daily Spokesman* is footing the finances?"

Deedra nodded. "Send your itemized bill there in care of Clete Bailey."

On the drive to the abbey, Deedra filled them in on all she knew about the missing Curt Ralston, the abbey's inhabitants and Sharlee Devon. "I think the delivery boy was captured up there somewhere and I'm afraid he might be dead by now."

Nick grimaced. "If he's dead he'll be harder to locate. Alive, we could set up surveillance on the abbey...maybe learn where he is because they would need to give him food and water. Dead, they could simply just avoid the burial place."

This brought on a gloomy silence.

Deke's voice finally broke that glum spell. "Tell us what you learned from Chuck Preston."

"Chuck told me he spent the most ghastly weekend of his life at the abbey. Certain important people wanted to know why Sharlee was incommunicado, and got one of Ricardo's invention manufacturers to get him an invite there. He was prevented from talking to Sharlee alone, says Ricardo has some holographic image ghost things cavorting about to scare visitors, and has a...ah...sister named Hannah, who acts as a housekeeper. She made his number one list of spooks. And he saw a mutant male there...and believes that Ricardo is a monster."

"Wow!" Deke remarked.

Just the mention of Chuck Preston's name gave the

situation credence. If Chuck said scary things were going on at the abbey then there were scary things going on there.

Nick just listened. Obviously he wasn't shaken by the vagaries of the human condition.

"You don't suppose old Ricardo kidnaps children for human experimentation?" Deke challenged.

"No," Nick answered. "We would have heard something about missing children within a few weeks or months after they moved there. I did a background check on their former place of residence. No record of missing children in that town, though there was a rumor that Ricardo had a mentally-challenged son somewhere. No one seemed to know the child's whereabouts, however. It's within the realm of possibility that this mutant is Ricardo's son who just grew to a gigantic size due to some birth defect."

They rounded the sharp curve and were suddenly in front of the narrow bridge where Deedra braked to a stop. They sat staring at the bridge a moment before getting out of the car.

Deke took pictures with his ever-present camera. Deedra had often thought that he cared more for that expensive camera than he did for her.

She pointed out where the electronic eye was located and showed them where she had landed when she dropped from the girders under the bridge.

Somewhere below them a rattlesnake buzzed.

"That damn snake is still angry at you, Deedra!" Deke remarked. There was a touch of awe in his voice. He stared into the ravine as if hypnotized.

Deedra saw movement on the far side of the bridge in the shadow of the trees. "I think Hannah has us under her scrutiny. She won't know why we are really here, though. She will probably think we are looking around and down into the ravine for the missing delivery boy. Let's just wander about a bit and then get in the car and leave."

Deke took one last photo hoping to catch a shot of Hannah in its focus.

"I've got a helicopter at the airstrip," Nick said. "Let's go fly around this area and get a closer look at the abbey and its grounds. It will give us an idea if there's another way to enter the abbey grounds and see if the boy's bicycle is around here. I doubt it. The other helicopter observers didn't find it. But they weren't looking specifically for a bicycle, they were looking for a boy in the ravine and only gave the abbey a cursory look."

They were silent during the drive to the airport. Deedra was surprised when Nick took the controls of the helicopter himself. It took only a few minutes to fly above the ancient abbey. It looked spooky even from the air.

Deedra pointed out the place where she was when Hannah hit her with the rock and also the rock wall along which she had moved though the darkness to reach the road. In places the wall was hidden from their view by the thick foliage.

The area to the east of the abbey was a surprise. A rough road wended through underbrush and old trees, finally connecting with a main road ten miles to the north of the abbey. The road had been traveled recently. It was not connected to the road leading to Bermondy that lay in front of the abbey. It was further east and behind the old buildings that were used as garages. Evidently the Embusteros left and returned to the abbey by way of that private road. An iron gate opened onto the road and looked as if it were unlocked. A tall fence surrounded the property behind the garages. Deedra hadn't seen it from the grounds.

Flying above the rough road that skirted the ravine they thought it doubtful anyone from Bermondy ever used it. Perhaps they were unaware of its existence.

"Looks like we found a way of approaching the abbey without alerting all those electronic gadgets," Nick remarked.

Nick swung the helicopter around the mountain and headed back over the abbey's grounds. They flew low enough to see the art studio and the summer-house sheltered in the heavy foliage. There was no sign of Hannah and no sign of movement around the house.

Nick swung the helicopter low over the ravine again. At the far end of the property, near the fence that ran behind the garages, was a faint trail leading up from the bottom of the canyon. Obviously an experienced climber could reach the abbey by climbing up at that point. Nick flew east along the ravine and over a small park where there were tables and benches. It was evidently a rest area for hikers. A well-worn path led off to the south away from the abbey.

"One would have to be a mountain goat to climb that trail up to the abbey," Deke muttered.

"It could be done. And who knows…it might be a way of escape at a crucial moment," Nick replied.

"Do you think Ricardo knows about that trail?" Deedra asked.

"I doubt it. Otherwise he would have taken more precaution near the edge there. He isn't the type to go for walks along the canyon rim anyway. But the mutant might. Anyway, we now know there are two ways of getting onto the abbey grounds without being detected. At least we can hope so."

"Do you think we stand any chance of getting Sharlee out of there alive?" Deke's voice sounded strained.

Deedra was again reminded of Deke and Sharlee's whirlwind romance several years earlier. Deedra was not aware of what had happened between them, she only recalled that it had been a very painful time for her. She had been very jealous of Sharlee then and was surprised that she had not remembered that jealousy until now. Perhaps, she mused, Sharlee had wanted marriage and Deke had not reciprocated. If she recalled events correctly, it wasn't long after their break-up that the wedding bells had rung out for Sharlee and Ricardo. Had Sharlee married Ricardo out of spite or on the rebound? Only the thought that Sharlee was rumored to be in love with Trent Kettering kept the green-eyed monster from rearing its ugly head again. Deedra's love for Deke was a very hurtful thing and jealousy was ever-present because of his refusal to commit to any kind of permanent relationship. And, she thought, as she stared into the ravine, the live-in situation he had wanted would never work. She would only settle for marriage.

Nick swooped over the abbey again and swung to the west nearer the archaic bridge. Flying low, they looked for signs of the boy's bicycle. As they hovered over the bridge Deedra imagined she could hear the buzz of rattlesnakes. The hairs on her neck tingled.

Nick swung back over the front lawns in hope of getting a glimpse of Sharlee. The windows were blank as if no life existed there.

"Deke, you didn't tell us what Trent Kettering had to say."

Deke frowned and sighed. It was as if he regretted

having to tell that there was another man in Sharlee's life.

"Trent is in love with Sharlee. He snuck up here several times to see her. This was before Sharlee was confined to the turret rooms. They met in that old summerhouse or down the road in an abandoned cabin. When Ricardo found out he tore the cabin down and locked up the summerhouse. After that he kept Sharlee locked up. If there's a child it's probably Trent Kettering's."

She saw that Deke's jaw was clenched. He evidently was struggling with the idea that Sharlee was actually committed to another man. She doubted that Deke was still in love with Sharlee, but assumed he would be very angry and frustrated to learn that an old reprobate like Ricardo was holding her captive. Deedra didn't blame Deke for wanting to help Sharlee. Any decent man would. And he would not be Deke if he didn't feel obligated to help her. Deke might take extremely dangerous chances to rescue Sharlee, but then he would tell her goodbye, perhaps not even take her into his arms. Suddenly Deedra realized that their shared profession caused Deke's consistent returning to her, because they had experienced adventures together. They had a common bond in their efforts to get the front-page stories. To him it wasn't a strong enough bond for him to marry her. She was definitely going to have to look for someone else, someone who wanted her as a wife and wanted her permanently.

"Kettering didn't know there was a child?" Deke asked.

"No. It was a shock, I think. He was all set to drive up here right then and there to ask Sharlee about the child. Trent was certain the child was his. Sharlee had told him that Ricardo didn't seem able to complete the sex act with her. Sharlee said she thought that his other wives had been so plain and ugly, her words not Trent's, that he just couldn't do anything but look at her, that he seemed afraid to touch her. I told Trent how Sharlee had thrown those notes out of the window. Trent panicked, ready to send in the National Guard. I had to really calm him down, actually restrained him for several minutes. Trent has a sharp temper. I persuaded him that any move on his part would only endanger both Sharlee and the child…and perhaps the missing Curt Ralston. When Trent calmed down I advised him to get an attorney, to get the legal stuff started down there. I was certain that a lawyer would also advise him against going to the abbey and demanding to see Sharlee. I told him it would just cause Sharlee and the baby unnecessary harm and he wouldn't want that on his conscience. No telling what Ricardo would do. I guess I scared him enough to wait. He agreed with the notion that Curt Ralston had turned up missing because of Ricardo."

"Trent did agree to stay away then?" Deedra asked.

"Reluctantly. Trent said he was going to get an attorney the next day. That would have been yesterday."

At that moment Nick pointed out another road. It was an abandoned logging road to the far south of the other road the Embusteros used. It ended at a place where tree stumps stood in witness to early logging, and was only a few hundred feet south and east of the abbey's front gates.

"We can park there where that old forest camp is, skirt the property to the east, and try to get onto the grounds through that gate behind the garages. It's no wonder people seldom saw Ricardo in town, he and Hannah simply drove off to another town north of Bermondy."

Nick swung the helicopter over the road once again while they scanned the thick brushy area for signs of the missing boy or his bicycle.

"Funny they haven't found that bicycle," Nick remarked. "It's usually the first sign of a missing child. How many times have we heard of the abandoned bicycle leading to tragic consequences?"

"What areas have been searched on foot?" Deke asked.

"I understand this roadside, along the lake shore and riverbanks, and in the ravine only closer to town.

R.D. said all the old buildings and sheds have been searched. They may drag the lake later, though there's no reason to think Curt's in it since he wasn't near the lake and the bicycle wasn't found there."

"You said the F.B.I. men went up to the abbey?"

"Yes. They didn't get to search it, of course. They did question Ricardo and he took them on a tour of the ground floor. I understand they saw Sharlee standing in an upstairs hall."

"You believe that Curt is hidden in the abbey, Deedra?" Nick challenged.

"Yes. I'm sure Curt went up there to find out more about Sharlee and to try and help her. You must remember Sharlee has been a glamorous movie star and everyone here in Bermondy has been wondering why she hasn't been seen in town anymore. Curt is an impressionable young boy, entering his teen years. It's reasonable to assume the he might have gone back to the abbey after finding that note for help from Sharlee. He would obviously want to help a beautiful woman like Sharlee. I think Hannah found Curt prowling around and took him back to the abbey."

"Why would they hold him though? It would make more sense for them to just scare him. Give him an ultimatum: stay away or else," Nick remarked.

Deedra had to admit that what Nick said was true. Still, it didn't change her belief that Curt's disappearance was in some way connected to the abbey; that he had gone there to try and help Sharlee.

Lack of fuel sent them back to the airstrip but they had learned what they wanted to know. They could always fly over the area again.

"You know, Nick, there's a gambling joint up in those mountains owned by Reuben Zolar. Do you think Curt might be up there?" Deedra suggested.

"Gambling? In this county?"

"No, not in this county. But they spend money here in Bermondy and Curt's father took a loan from Zolar to start his bank here."

"Is that right?" Nick sounded stunned. "I'll bet no one has searched up there!"

"Couldn't get a warrant because it's in a different jurisdiction."

"Do you really think they would kidnap Curt?" Nick challenged. "If I understand it, Zolar wants to keep his presence up there quiet—no trouble, no adverse publicity. I'm sure the F.B.I. knows all about his operation. And if they haven't made an effort to get a search warrant they probably don't think Curt is anywhere near there. There's been no ransom note. That would be the first thing those gangsters would do if they were holding him. If there weren't any money to gain from it they wouldn't expend the effort. Murder isn't on their agenda, at least not the murder of a young boy. They are quite aware of what happens when a child is missing. It stirs up the public like nothing else. If they go after other mobsters the public just doesn't give a damn."

"Looks like R.D. has company," Deke remarked as he observed the sheriff's patrol car that was parked in front of the newspaper's office.

"I'm anxious to talk to this sheriff. His hands are tied in the matter of Sharlee's…ah…captivity," Deedra said. "Nick, just remember that you are just another news reporter."

Nick grinned a lopsided grin that was his most endearing trait. "Yeah. I don't think anyone would take me for an investigator, do you?"

Deedra smiled.

Evidently Deke was still thinking about Sharlee or something they weren't privy to because he didn't laugh or comment. It was as if he hadn't heard a word Nick said.

"There is a Nicholas Milford that works at our paper. You could always say you were he if anyone asks. Even if the sheriff checks, the paper would tell them that such a person works there." Deedra laughed to herself. There was no comparison between the men. The Nicholas at the newspaper would feel put down. He was quite the ladies' man, tall and handsome.

The sheriff gave Deedra her own surprise. Why she had expected a man of medium traits, she didn't know. Rex Walling was over six feet tall and had hair that curled around his head. His light brown eyes could easily darken with anger. He was lithe as if he exercised every day, and obviously thought of himself as macho. And he was no fool.

"Any news of the boy?" Nick asked.

The sheriff turned his attention to Nick, looked him up and down, and evidently didn't perceive that he was a detective. From now on, Deedra mused, Rex Walling would think of Nick as a reporter.

She caught the glint in Nick's eyes and knew he had enjoyed giving the sheriff the wrong impression. She wasn't sure, however, that it was wise to make an enemy of this man. Rex Walling didn't give the impression of a placid personality and Deedra suspected he would not make a pleasant adversary.

TEN

SHERIFF WALLING continued talking to R.D. "There are just no clues to Curt's disappearance. Since we haven't found his bicycle, there's a chance he was snatched by a passing motorist. If that's it, if some porno freak got him, we'll probably never find him."

Nick was taking pictures of the sheriff with his watch camera. It was a device Deedra thought of as a dirty little snoop, though she knew the C.I.A. and other investigators used them frequently.

Deke stepped up to the sheriff. "Have the F.B.I. men learned anything, found any clues?"

The sheriff started. "What F.B.I. men?"

"Sorry, thought they had clued you in. In kidnapping cases they are always notified. I guess the banker contacted them."

The sheriff was understandably disturbed at not having been alerted about their entering the case. He had been out leading search parties for Curt all day and no one had bothered to inform him. "Since," he said tersely, "we aren't sure this is a kidnapping, it is still under my jurisdiction. I am, however," he sighed, "grateful for their help and the resources at their command." Rex Walling strode out with more machismo than he felt.

"Hey! That wasn't kosher for the federal boys to ignore the sheriff like that!" R.D. objected.

"I think the federal men just didn't want to call attention to their presence in town before it was necessary," Deedra soothed.

R.D., it seemed, was very loyal to the people of Bermondy. She noted earlier that he was seldom critical of anyone in Bermondy, and had been slightly reluctant to tell her anything about Sandy Harris.

"Did the sheriff," Deke threw Deedra an amused glance, "search the grounds around the abbey?"

"No," R.D. answered. "Rex went up there, but Ricardo refused to let him search inside or around the grounds. The judge told him there wasn't any evidence that Curt had been there, so refused to give him a warrant. Rex Walling was really miffed and got uppity. The judge replied that they would probably find Curt's body floating in the lake."

R.D. was getting more and more depressed over Curt's disappearance. Deedra thought he probably blamed himself for including the abbey in the boy's delivery route.

Deke scratched his head. "What does the sheriff really think?"

"He's almost convinced that some porno freak

kidnapped the boy. Curt's a very handsome lad just entering his teens. Porno bait, the sheriff called it."

"Do you think the F.B.I. has any special reason for not notifying the sheriff of their presence here in Bermondy?" She asked Nick in a low voice that R.D. couldn't overhear.

"I don't think it means anything. Unless they are actively hunting for someone, they don't always tell the locals they are in town. You want to remember they don't go around in uniforms to alert the unwary. Some people are put off by uniforms and won't tell everything they know, but they would to a man in a business suit with a badge and a manner of authority. Especially if it's with the authority of the federal government. What happens when a uniformed officer goes to the door of a residence? Every neighbor is instantly curious. No, I don't think the sheriff should feel put out. Until this morning, the missing boy wasn't publicized anyway."

"What," Deedra asked R.D., "did Rex Walling think about the note I retrieved?"

R.D. sighed. "He wasn't surprised. Ricardo had told him that Sharlee had a baby, and had her show it to him. It's that fact that convinced him there wasn't anything criminal going on up there. Rex didn't know about Hannah, however."

"I don't see how anyone can fault the sheriff," Nick continued, "Many law men suspect that criminal type things are going on, but are hampered by laws that keep them from doing anything about it. In this case, it's the lack of a search warrant."

"Agreed," Deedra sighed.

"What kind of a guy is this Rex Walling anyway?" Deke growled.

Deedra was still smiling when she said to Nick, "Deke doesn't take to other handsome men like the sheriff."

Nick grinned. "I wouldn't think that Deke would have serious competition from anyone."

"That's just it. He usually doesn't. But suddenly there's Trent Kettering in the background and Rex Walling walking around in a uniform. Women like men in uniforms."

Deke stared at her as if he hadn't heard her correctly and Deedra felt a twinge of guilt for baiting him.

"Let's go out and talk to that woman who lives at the edge of town," Nick suggested to soothe Deke's put-down. "What's her name again?"

"Mrs. Seltzer. She lives there alone. She's about seventy, seventy-five years old," Deedra replied.

Mrs. Seltzer was sitting on the front porch. "I knew you news people would be calling on me soon. What is it you want to know?"

"You saw and talked to Curt Ralston that Wednesday afternoon?" Deke asked.

"Yes. He always spoke if I was on the porch. Most times he got off his bike and handed the newspaper to me instead of just throwing it onto the porch. Curt knew his manners, was taught them by responsible parents, and he was a very bright boy."

"Why do you speak of him in the past tense?" Deedra's heart was thumping.

"I think he's dead! Otherwise he would be home where he belongs. Curt wasn't one to run around like some boys his age. Curt never gave his parents a moment of grief."

"Did he talk about anything special that day?" Deedra asked.

"Those F.B.I. men asked me that. No, he just seemed like usual—friendly. He asked me if there were any errands that I would like to have him do for me. Talked about how he was going to buy a new mountain bike with his paper earnings. Curt did ask me if I knew Sharlee Devon, who lives up at the old abbey. I asked him why he wanted to know. Curt said he delivered papers there and had seen Sharlee Devon standing at the window several times. Then he told me he thought the Embusteros had a baby because he had seen Sharlee holding a baby up to the window."

This was indeed news. Curt had known about the baby. Who else had he told? Perhaps he and Sharlee had more contact than anyone knew. If Curt were in the habit of asking this old lady if she needed any errands done, he would certainly have responded to a younger more famous lady's request. Had Sharlee asked him to do something for her and Ricardo had found out?

"I asked Curt if he was sure it was a baby, that there were reports that Sharlee was kind of ill. He said no, he had seen the baby move, and had heard it cry. Curt said he thought she was very unhappy living there and he thought that her husband didn't let her go outside."

"Why did Curt think Sharlee wasn't allowed to go outside?"

"I don't know. I thought maybe Curt had talked to her. He was plainly worried about her, had her on his mind. If she had asked Curt for help, I'm sure Curt would have done all he could to help her. No matter what that was."

"Then Curt might have gone up to the abbey and tried to get in, or prowled about the grounds. He might even have talked to her if Sharlee had opened a window."

Mrs. Seltzer sighed. "I'm sure he would. Curt was always ready to help anyone. And if Curt thought Sharlee Devon was in real need of help, I'm sure he would have made some attempt to find out what she needed and how he could help her."

They exchanged glances. It was the same theory Deedra had suggested.

"Curt didn't leave Bermondy that afternoon then?" Deedra sighed, knowing the answer, but wanting Nick to hear it.

"No, not before dusk anyway. I couldn't say who left after I went inside the house and it got dark. But I'm certain Curt wouldn't leave town without letting his parents know."

They thanked Mrs. Seltzer and drove back into town.

"Let's drive out that old logging road. We can circle the house from there by crossing to the north of the abbey," Nick suggested.

They left Deedra's car in the thickets near the forest camp and scrambled through brush and brambles until they were in sight of the abbey. Even from that distance it had a haunted look.

"That place really gives me the creeps!" Deedra remarked.

"Anyone know why Ricardo bought that old monstrosity?" Nick asked.

"Not really. Ricardo stated at the time that it was a perfect place for his lab and that any noises or disturbances he made would not bother any neighbors. Everyone is puzzled about why Sharlee agreed to live there. Especially since she had been living the good life in and around Hollywood."

"I think," Deke suggested, "that he just doesn't want anyone interfering in Sharlee's life. I think he's a very possessive man. His money and fame bought him a prize, a young woman that most men desired. I don't think he's deeply in love with her or he certainly wouldn't treat her like that. I think he just regards her as another of his possessions."

Deedra nodded. "That was certainly the impression I got when I went up there. It was like Sharlee was an inanimate possession, not a real person."

"Sounds creepy," Nick remarked.

"Believe me, it is creepy, all in capital letters."

"You must have received a scare then?" Nick grinned.

"You bet I did! If Ricardo is as crazy as I think he is, Sharlee Devon hasn't a chance of escaping unless we can do something to help her. You've already heard what the law has done. They are helpless at this point to intercede. Sharlee would have to swear out a complaint, and how can she do that when she can't even get out of the house? And even then Ricardo could get a smart lawyer to say she is mentally unfit."

Into the momentary silence that followed, Deedra added, "Another thing. If it weren't for those inventions, I wouldn't believe this was the same Ricardo. Even Sandy Harris said his personality changed suddenly. His looks are slightly different than those taken in the photo of their wedding. There is a streak of white hair down the very middle of his head. Almost looks like an animal. I found nothing friendly about him and everyone says that Ricardo is friendly. Rather charming, in fact. He would have had to be to attract Sharlee in the first place. She isn't likely to have chosen a grump when she had the pick of several men." Out of the corner of her eye she saw Deke clench his fists.

The road ended near a thatch of wild brambles almost opposite the front gates. They hid behind the brambles peering at the abbey whose ancient structure loomed into the air as if reaching for the clouds. The crenellated turret gave it an even more medieval look, ancient and desolate. There was nothing about those blank windows that suggested life went on inside.

Deke stared at the turret windows.

Deedra knew that he was hoping for a glimpse of Sharlee. Again she wondered about his feelings for her. What if it had been Sharlee, and not Deke, that had put an end to their relationship? What did Deke think knowing that Sharlee had chosen to marry a man like Ricardo after dating a man of Deke's caliber? She knew that Deke was puzzling over it, wondered if he felt even the slightest guilt over their break-up?

Beside her Nick muttered, "In a place that size, the Ralston boy could be kept for days and even weeks without being found. They could just keep moving him from room to room and then to the sub-cellars.

It would take a battalion of men just to search it all at the same time and make certain they didn't move him. The cellars are what bother me. Do you know how they can be entered?"

"Yes. Sandy said there is a way in from the kitchen and one from the hallway near the turret stairs, but she thought Ricardo had boarded them up. The construction men didn't attempt to change the cellars because the cost would have been prohibitive. No telling what is down there."

"I've a hunch Ricardo bought this abbey with its spacious grounds for the mutant. It's really perfect for that. He could roam around the grounds and live in the cellars, and he would bother no one. And it's a good place to hide Hannah. How Ricardo got Sharlee to go along with that is the mystery. He might have told her this was to be her castle; that she would be queen here. And Sharlee probably planned on entertaining all of her Hollywood friends here. Ricardo could have painted quite a different picture of what life would be like in 'the castle.' Nick paused a moment.

"He probably told Sharlee that she could have all sorts of things here. Like a huge swimming pool, tennis courts, the works. And with all those rooms Sharlee could have planned weekend guests and spectacular parties."

"I think you're right, Nick. And you have to remember that the price was right also. They couldn't have been asking much for the property since it had been empty for years…and with its lurid reputation. If you recall, Sharlee's marriage was very romantic— the eccentric millionaire taking Sharlee off to her own castle. I think the Hollywood reporters even played up that angle," Deedra reminded.

This caused Deke to grimace. He seemed even more morose. Whatever thoughts roamed through his mind, Deke kept to them to himself. Was his old passion for Sharlee being rekindled by her desperate plight? Would the possibility of rescuing Sharlee from that old monastery present a romantic twist that would appeal to Deke? Deedra couldn't help feeling a slight resentment towards Sharlee.

They moved northward to a place where they could see Ricardo's lab. The drapes were drawn, and if Ricardo was in there no light showed to indicate it. The windows of the upper rooms were just dull lifeless panes.

"Look there," Nick pointed, "there's a large cellar, see the windows near the foundation? Did Sandy Harris draw a sketch of the cellars?"

"No, she never went down there."

"There's got to be an outside entrance. Let's see if we can locate it."

They scurried through brambles until reaching the edge of the ravine. The trail up the cliff's side was steep, but more passable than it had looked from the air. There was no indication of anyone's passage, nothing to tell them if Curt Ralston might have climbed it. And they couldn't see any cellar entrance.

Nick looked puzzled. "I should think there would be an entrance near the kitchen, surely in the old days they stored vegetables and wine down there."

There was a squeaking noise as Hannah emerged through the back door and put garbage into a large container. A frown serrated her forehead. She walked toward the ravine, peered into the foliage that grew along the edge, and then peered into the ravine itself. Hannah glanced about again, shrugged in a frustrated way, and returned to the house.

"Whew!" Nick exclaimed. "Something has put the wind up. Hannah is certainly suspicious. The thing is, did the F.B.I.'s visit cause it or does she know what happened to Curt Ralston?"

Beside her Deke muttered, "God, that woman looks like the wicked witch! I wonder where she parks her broom?"

"Let's get out of here before we're discovered. If Curt is still alive in there, our presence endangers him. If Hannah should see us there would be hell to pay!"

They didn't leave any too soon. Ricardo opened the front door, went down the steps and stared about as if he, too, expected to find someone there. He then strode to the end of the driveway and looked up and down the road. He hesitated as if he thought he had missed something. Obviously uneasy, he returned to the house.

"Don't move!" Nick whispered.

Sure enough, Ricardo appeared at the front window and continued to stare outside as if looking for movement of some kind.

"Look," Deke murmured, "Sharlee is standing at the upstairs window. I think she sees us."

Just then they saw Sharlee wave and clasp her hands together as if praying. They knew she was asking for help.

Hidden behind the foliage they waved back.

Ricardo remained at the window, a dark angry look on his face.

Sharlee vanished from sight. They remained where they were until at last Ricardo turned away from the window. Even then they waited for several minutes to move. Ricardo didn't reappear so they hurried to the car.

On the way back to Bermondy, Deedra reminded them that Ricardo had invited her to visit again, that he would have information about another invention. "I'll be able to show him the feature article Clete had printed up several days ago."

"You mean," Deke asked, "that Clete had a story ready before you even went up there?"

"Yep. Don't say we don't plan our moves."

"I don't suppose Ricardo would let you do a feature on Sharlee?" Deke asked.

Deedra gave him a rueful look.

"No, I'm sure he wouldn't. Right now Ricardo doesn't want the world to know about that baby."

"At least you'll have an excuse to be there if Hannah finds you prowling around," Deke remarked.

"I doubt if he would call it an excuse unless I went marching right up to the front door. He and Hannah are certainly skittish. It's like they're expecting people to prowl around."

Nick, who hadn't voiced an opinion in several minutes, said, "Now wait a minute. Ricardo might give you an interview if he thought that would take the pressure off—if he could give you the impression that Curt Ralston wasn't there. You have a printed article for him. What better excuse than to deliver it? It would certainly please his inflated ego. Ricardo is all wrapped up in Ricardo. What I'd like to know is what is Hannah doing there, and why does Ricardo want her there? Ricardo obviously wants the world to think Sharlee is ill…it's an excuse for Hannah's presence…a simple explanation, but is it really why she's there, or is there another reason?"

Deedra glanced at Nick. It was amazing how his mind went right to the crux of the matter. If there was one thing Nick understood, it was the criminal mind.

She glanced at Deke who had remained strangely

silent. She noted that the glimpse of Sharlee had really shaken him. Sharlee had looked frail and ill…and helpless. Faint perspiration covered Deke's forehead.

Pangs of jealousy hit Deedra once again and she felt depression set in as they returned to the newspaper's office.

Curt's bicycle had been found in a thicket just south of Bermondy. The F.B.I. had organized a search of the area. They were now making an intense search of the underbrush and R.D. had gone off to join them.

On learning this Deke and Nick went off to help in the search.

Deedra sighed and decided it was an opportunity to talk to Kortney Vickers. "Have you always lived in Bermondy?"

"Yes, I was born here. Guess I'm stuck here." There was a tinge of bitterness in her voice. "Tell me, what's it like working for a big city newspaper?"

Deedra told her what a typical day was like and how exciting it was to be in on the big news stories.

"Did you ever want to be a TV news anchor?" Kortney asked.

"No. I don't like to be that confined. Those people have to adhere to strict ground rules, have to be more objective, have to be very careful about not offending anyone. It just isn't my cup of tea, and I don't have a good television appearance. I don't like having people recognize me wherever I go. Sometimes they do, but most of the time they simply don't care who I am or what I'm doing because they have a life. The ones who don't seem to live vicariously through people who lead more exciting lives."

Deedra paused. "Do you think you would like to work for a big city newspaper?"

"Yes. It's what I dream about. I just want to get out of Bermondy!"

"Have you ever talked to Sharlee Devon?"

The girl's eyes widened in surprise at the sudden change of subject.

"Yes! When she first moved here. She invited me to visit her, but when I went up there, Ricardo wouldn't let me in. He said Sharlee was ill, that she wasn't seeing anyone."

"What is your impression of Ricardo?"

"He's just crazy! I can't imagine what Sharlee saw in him to actually marry that man! Surely money can't be that important!" Distaste and disgust clouded Kortney's pretty features.

ELEVEN

"Do you know Sandy Harris, the doctor's wife?" Deedra asked Kortney.

"Yes." Kortney didn't elaborate and Deedra received the impression that Kortney either didn't like Sandy or didn't know her very well.

After a few moments, Deedra volunteered, "I visited Sandy at her house, the one called Land's End. My, they certainly have a beautiful home."

"Yes, I've been there a couple of times. I guess Sandy's modeling career helped pay for it." Was there a trace of envy in Kortney's voice?

Deedra felt it expedient to change the subject.

"Is there any kind of social activity here in Bermondy? Like a country club, for instance?"

"Not in Bermondy. The local Women's Club is the only thing approaching the social set and it's open to everyone in town. No real lines are drawn here. You might find Dr. Harris out on the golf course golfing with the local mechanic or storeowner. Practically everyone who lives in Bermondy was born here. They all know everything about everyone."

"So you might be the only person who really wants to leave Bermondy?"

She blushed. "Yes. There isn't anyone who understands that."

"Are you in love with R.D.?"

She blushed. "Yes, I guess I am. He is very discreet and quite reserved. I don't know what to think about him. It's almost as if he is afraid of marriage. Though why, I can't imagine. His parents were one of the happiest couples that ever lived in Bermondy."

"Is he involved with anyone now?"

Kortney shook her head. "I haven't heard of him dating anyone."

"Has R.D. been involved in the past?"

Kortney sighed. "Yes, I think there was someone, I don't recall who it was, though. I was just in high school at the time and wasn't interested in R.D. then."

At dusk the men returned. They hadn't found Curt's body and no evidence that suggested he had ever been in that area. The F.B.I. men thought his bicycle had been dumped there. They really gave the bike a look-see to determine whether a car had hit it. But the bicycle only had a few dents made from being tossed into the brush. They determined that a man had been the culprit because the bike was too heavy for a woman to manage.

"Now that the bike has been found, the federal

boys have concluded that the boy is dead." Deke said. Then he suggested another theory. "I think the bicycle is a plant. It obviously wasn't hit by a car. Someone placed it far away from where Curt actually is to prevent a more intense search of that immediate area. It's probably a way of lulling suspicion, but it doesn't clear Ricardo, who is strong enough to have taken the bicycle there. Even Hannah could accomplish that by the size and strength of her. If Curt had gone back after delivering the papers and either Ricardo or Hannah saw him, his fate was sealed. He's probably hidden in the cellars under the abbey."

Deke paused then added, "It would be expedient for them to get rid of the bicycle so they wouldn't have to answer any questions about it." Deke sighed and paused again. "Remember, Mrs. Seltzer hinted that Curt might have gone back to the abbey to help Sharlee. Curt actually told Mrs. Seltzer about Sharlee and her baby. He never told his parents and he didn't confide in his friends. When his parents were told about the note it was the first time they had heard about Curt's interest in Sharlee. If they had known, they probably would have put the abbey off limits, would have made him promise not to go there anymore. And from what we've heard about Curt, he wouldn't want to make that promise."

Deedra stared at Deke. Where had he been when she had espoused that very theory? Had Deke been so caught up in Sharlee's predicament that Curt's disappearance hadn't involved his thinking?

"Yes, I've talked to several of the boys and none of them have any idea where Curt might have gone. He never went around bragging about the fact that he wasn't afraid to deliver papers at the abbey…and he wasn't. If Curt planned to help Sharlee, none of the boys knew about it," R.D. confirmed.

"There's nothing more we can do tonight," Deke sighed. He glanced at Deedra. "Tomorrow we'll search the area around where you parked your car, Deedra. We might be able to cross the arroyo and scale that rock wall. Maybe we can get onto the grounds that way."

"Can I get you to help out here, Deedra, so I can join the search?" R.D. asked.

"Yes. I need to get some copy off to Clete anyway."

"Let's find a restaurant and get dinner. You want to join us, R.D.?" Deke invited.

"Sorry, I have some work to do here." He glanced at Kortney. If she noticed, she gave no sign of it.

"Let's go, I'm starving!" Deedra led the way.

They dined at the Bermondy House restaurant. It was Bermondy's only claim to sophistication. The lowered lights, intimate settings and candles gave it a clandestine atmosphere.

Deedra was depressed. Deke was obviously in

turmoil over Sharlee, but there was something more emotional to his glumness. Deedra wondered if she was always going to have to compete with Deke's other women. Then recalled her vow to start looking for Mr. Right somewhere else.

Deke must have sensed her feelings. Despite Nick's presence he said, "Deedra, you know you are still my best girl!"

Deedra blushed and glanced at Nick.

"Don't mind me!" Nick grinned.

But Nick's presence stifled the personal moment and it slipped away.

"We've got to come up with a plan to get Sharlee out of there," Deke said, agitated.

"That could get us into serious trouble," Deedra reminded.

"Not if we can take her directly to a judge, have her swear out a complaint," Nick replied. "But getting her out of there is going to be something we'll have to do without the help of the law." Nick gulped a swallow of coffee as if he really needed it. "That child is the unknown factor. How old is he? Can he be quiet during an escape attempt? Can he even walk or would he have to be carried?"

Deke groaned, put his hands to his head. "Let's forget all this for a while. I've got to think of something else. Deedra, what have you been doing for excitement since solving the murders at The Dunes in Heywood?"

They all laughed and it served to release their stress. They inveigled Nick into telling them about some of his investigative experiences. All too soon the meal was over. Nick decided to retire early and left them to return to his motel room.

"Where are you staying, Deke?"

"I don't have a room yet. You don't have an extra bed in your motel room, do you?"

"I have a couch, but you've got to behave."

He grinned. "I always behave. I behave like myself."

"You know what I mean, Deke. I don't want to get really involved again. Not unless you are ready for marriage, that is."

Deke looked at her, but didn't reply. He was silent all the way to the motel.

After they had both showered, Deedra offered to make coffee.

"Sounds great. I need to tell you about Sharlee and me."

Deedra felt a stab of fear. Then she realized it was better to get it out, to find out just what this was going to mean in her own private life.

At first Deke was hesitant as if he couldn't find the words to adequately explain himself. It was a sad story, one of lust and passion, and Sharlee's evidence of possessiveness. Sharlee had wanted Deke to give up his career and manage hers. She had wanted him at her beck and call. Deke had rebelled. He was far too independent for anything like that. Deedra could almost hear the words Deke used to set Sharlee straight. It had broken up their relationship. Several months later there were rumors Sharlee was seeing a young movie producer. At that time Deke hadn't known his name. The next thing he heard was that Sharlee had married Ricardo Embustero. That had shocked him as nothing else had in his relationships with women. He finished the narrative with, "and now she's in trouble and I've no choice but to help her. I don't want to get involved with her again, though. She would probably still want the same things. I can't give up my life's work or my lifestyle for her."

"She's involved with Trent Kettering and his baby son right now anyway," Deedra reminded.

"Yes," he breathed as if that was an answer to a prayer.

"Now, where do we stand, Deke?"

"You know the answer to that, Deedra. I love you, but I can't seem to cope with the thought of marriage. I know that on trips to cover news stories I'd meet someone and have a fling. That's just me. You would be home waiting and miserable because you would know what I was doing. It just wouldn't work."

Deedra sighed. "You know, Deke, that I want

children. My biological clock is going to run out one
of these days. I am going to start looking for someone
else. I need the security of marriage. I need a family.
I do love you, and I am always going to want you, but
I am not going to wait forever."

Deke pulled her into his arms. As usual, Deedra
returned his kisses. They spent a romantic and un-
forgettable evening but Deke spent the night on the
couch.

"I have enough complications in my life, Deke,
without adding you to the list," Deedra told him.

The next day Deke and Nick went to join the search
for Curt Ralston and Deedra was left on her own.
She went to the newspaper office to tell R.D. that she
intended to go out to the abbey again. "The old man
invited me, you know. I want to show him this article
Clete prepared. Perhaps I'll get a chance to talk to
Sharlee."

"Deedra, I don't think that's very wise. Remember,
Hannah is on guard now." R.D. looked worried.

"I'll be careful. If I drive up there just like I have
a right to, I don't think they'll do anything. And I'll
tell Ricardo that I've told my boss I intend to deliver
the article today. That will keep them from trying to
kill me anyway. I promise not to take unnecessary
chances."

R.D.'s anxious frown was an unspoken warning.

It was a clear, hot day. The heat clung tenaciously

in the canyon areas between the mountains with scarcely a breeze to relieve it. Once again Deedra was glad she lived near the ocean where fresh breezes cooled the days and allowed one to sleep at night.

SHE PASSED THE AREA of the men's search. Cars lined the road on the Bermondy side of the bridge. Several men were searching through the brushy areas on both sides of the road. Deedra crossed the narrow bridge, wondering if it rang a warning bell up at the abbey.

Suddenly she shuddered. What made her think she could help Sharlee? Was R.D. right in advising her against making a trip to the abbey? Whatever. She was driving right up to the old place and must at least go up to the front door.

Ricardo and Hannah were both looking out a downstairs window. She caught a glimpse of Sharlee in the far corner window of the turret. She was holding a baby in her arms.

Deedra bounded up the stairs, the newspaper in her hands. When Ricardo opened the door, she handed it to him.

"This is the feature story about you, Mr. Embustero. I drove out here to give it to you the minute I received it from my boss. I hope you like it." She smiled at him. It took effort.

Hannah was lurking in the dark hall behind him.

"I wondered what brought you out here. Do you

know what those people are doing alongside the road on the other side of my property?" He growled with no thanks for the newspaper article.

"I understand they are searching for that missing boy, Curt Ralston. His bicycle was found yesterday. They searched that area at the south end of town. They've searched almost everywhere now. The sheriff thinks he might have drowned in the lake and there is talk of dragging it."

"Are you referring to the missing boy the F.B.I. men were here asking about?" Ricardo stared at her.

"Yes. He's the only missing boy, isn't he?" She saw Hannah turn and scurry down the hall.

Ricardo cleared his throat. "I think so, yes. It is a shame for a handsome young lad like that to simply disappear. I suppose there are all kinds of news people in town now."

"Yes. The F.B.I. and several other law people have come to search. The parents haven't received a ransom note so they don't think the boy was kidnapped."

"Are you covering that story?" Ricardo growled, his black eyes boring into hers.

"I am now. If the boy hadn't disappeared I would have gone back to the city right after my interview with you. Now that I'm on the scene, my boss wants me to stay rather than send someone else up here. I'm afraid this story is going to have a sad ending."

"Yes. Well, thank you for bringing this newspaper article out to me. I haven't yet completed the invention that I spoke to you about. I have run into a snag and it might take longer than I had planned on."

"Oh! Well, that's all right. You can reach me at the newspaper. The address is on the paper there." She turned away as if to leave, then asked, "Is your wife feeling better now?"

The question seemed to startle him. "Ah, yes. She is better. However, these things take time."

"Give her my best," Deedra said as she turned and hurried down the steps. She climbed into her car and looked up just in time to see Sharlee waving from the window.

Hannah was scowling through a window near the west side of the house. Ricardo stood in the open doorway waiting for her to leave.

When Deedra reached the end of the drive and the car was on the road, she stopped and took pictures of the abbey. Fortunately, Sharlee was standing at the window with the baby in her arms. Ricardo stared out of a downstairs window and then turned away.

Deedra knew he was going to check on Sharlee.

She took a few more photos but Sharlee had vanished. The pictures would prove that Sharlee had a baby. She had hoped to get a photo of Hannah. Until Deedra's arrival no one had seemed to know of Hannah's existence except Chuck Preston. Now, though, both Deke and Nick had seen her and both agreed that she had probably been the source of the ghost stories.

At the bridge she stopped and took more photos. She made sure to get one of the electronic eye gadgets. She then drove on to the place where the search was taking place.

The men hadn't turned up any clues. There was a place where the bushes had been trampled down, but nothing else significant. A wild animal could have done that, or even children at play, though this area was out of bounds for most children. The searchers were discouraged and most of them were ready to abandon the search. They were beginning to believe the sheriff was right in thinking that the boy had been kidnapped.

The sheriff had climbed down into the canyon and found nothing. He walked up to her car. "It's like that kid disappeared into thin air. We've searched everywhere except inside the old abbey, and I'd do that if the law allowed it. I don't understand why Ricardo Embustero doesn't let us just look around. It looks suspicious when they won't cooperate, like they have something to hide. Most people would go out of their way to help locate a missing child."

"Well," Deedra drawled, "Ricardo and Hannah aren't most people. They have to be the strangest couple I have ever met. Ricardo wanted to know what all this activity over here was about. I told him. He asked me if I was referring to the missing boy the F.B.I. had talked to him about. I said it was the only missing boy, wasn't it? That sent Hannah skittering toward the back of the house. I don't know what that action meant…whether Hannah didn't want to be asked questions or that she was frightened about something."

"Ricardo didn't let you talk to Sharlee Devon?" Sheriff Rex Walling's brown eyes were clouded with worry.

"No. And he didn't invite me in. Ricardo said he would get in touch with me when his new invention was completed. I did see Sharlee at a window holding the baby and got a photo of them from the road."

"I talked to Ricardo about Sharlee again," the sheriff told her. "I told him I'd been getting a number of inquiries about her from Hollywood and other places. He said that since the birth of their child, Sharlee had suffered a depression that left her frail and sometimes ill. He said that on the advice of a doctor, he allowed Sharlee to roam about the turret, but that she was to have no visitors at this time. He said she had even repapered some of the walls up there and that he felt she was gradually getting better. She didn't want to see people, didn't want them see how thin and frail she looked. It would be bad for her image. Ricardo seems to have all the answers. And they do make sense. No one can force Sharlee to appear in public. Of course, we don't know if that's Sharlee's wish or Ricardo's, and there's no way of proving that right now."

"You're beginning to wonder," Deedra guessed, "like most of us do, if the boy is being held captive in the abbey. Perhaps in those cellars. If Curt died there, no one would ever learn of it."

The sheriff ran a hand over his weary face. "Yes, that's what I think. But what can I do? If the F.B.I. can't get in there it stands to reason that I can't. The only way we're ever going to learn if he's there is for someone to just go in there and look. And I think that's near to impossible." The sheriff gave her a steady look as if he was aware that she, Nick and Deke were planning to do just that.

Deedra looked away, not wanting Rex Walling to see that he was right. "You've asked the Nevada authorities to check out that gambling place in the mountains?" she asked.

"Yes. Reuben Zolar let the F.B.I. search everywhere up there. Of course, they had to ignore the gambling apparatus because that was in the agreement that allowed them to search. I think it amused Reuben to know that the law people couldn't do anything about it, and that they knew it."

"So that theory is out. Tell me, Sheriff, how would you go about getting into the old abbey?"

The sheriff gave her a wry grin. "Me? I can't plan on doing anything like that!"

"I know, but if you could, how would you?" Deedra challenged.

The sheriff shrugged. It was obvious that he wasn't going to endanger his job.

While they stood there talking, most of the searchers had returned to their cars and driven away. Just the sheriff and Deedra were left standing there.

Deedra glanced toward the old bridge. "Look at that!"

A giant man was standing at the edge of Ricardo's property, staring at them. He was at least seven feet tall. His shoulders were huge and his long, straggly hair hung down below them. He returned their stares and then turned, clumsily lumbering away.

"I can't believe I just saw that!" the sheriff exclaimed.

"You did though. That's the basis for those stories of a Frankenstein monster up here. Now, Sheriff, I asked you how you would go about getting into the abbey if you could. I know the law says you can't, but if you could, how would you do it?"

The sheriff's eyes narrowed to slits. There was grim determination settling in on his usually placid features. "I would try to get into the house first by sneaking in the back door. I'm pretty sure they don't keep it locked during the day. I'd look in the downstairs rooms for the boy. Then I'd go up to the turret rooms. I'd look in the cellars last. As kids we used to dare each other to go down there. No one was brave enough to go down into the cellars, though we did roam about the abbey a bit. If I remember correctly, there's an entrance to the cellar from the kitchen or porch with steps leading down so you don't have to go outside to reach the basement area. I'm not certain, it's been a long time and they may have boarded those entrances up when they remodeled. They called it remodeling, but from what I saw, they just removed a few partitions to give Ricardo a bigger lab. The layout was very similar to what I recall from the time we teenagers took a look around inside. Scary damn place! We only went inside the abbey once. We never had any desire or curiosity to go there again, though we often sneaked around the grounds. We just silently agreed not to ever go inside again. I guess you've heard about the abbey's reputation?"

TWELVE

DEEDRA AND THE SHERIFF went over the details of the reported "haunting" of the abbey.

"Who do you think that mutant boy is?" Deedra asked.

"I have no idea."

"My sources tell me that Ricardo Embustero had a son when he lived in the East," Deedra began. "No one in the town of his former residence seems to know just where the boy is now. Some people think that Ricardo bought the old abbey for a place to raise the boy because he thought he would grow into an unnaturally giant size. There was a check done where Ricardo lived and no children were reported missing there."

"You are thorough, aren't you?"

"We have to make sure of our facts. Can't risk libel. Our paper is very skittish about that," Deedra replied.

"I've got to admit that strange things have been happening around this town since Ricardo moved here. I've investigated more complaints about strange things going on out on this road lately than ever before. It used to be the local teenage necking place. Now, the young people avoid this area like they would a plague."

"I think that's wise, don't you? I wouldn't want to meet that mutant or Hannah in the dark!"

The sheriff nodded agreement.

"I want to tell you something. Ricardo has that bridge bugged. It has some kind of an electronic gadget on it at the far end near his property. It alerts him to visitors in the area. They also have a surveillance camera or something on the front gates. It's all right for him to put one there, but isn't it illegal for him to bug that bridge?"

"Yep. He can't legally do that."

"Shall we go over and dismantle it, or do you want to wait and let the F.B.I. men do it? Tell them you discovered it today?"

The sheriff gave her a doubtful look and then smiled. "What are you planning to do?"

"I wouldn't want to put you in the position of knowing someone was trespassing, Sheriff. So I can't tell you what I am planning to do, if anything."

Deedra turned to walk toward her car and saw the mutant again. He was below them in the area the men had just searched, and he was shaking his fist at them.

"Look there," she pointed, "how did he get across that arroyo to this side? There's got to be a way near the back of the property. Let's watch and see what he does."

They stood beside Deedra's car and watched the mutant. He seemed undecided about what to do next. Presently they saw him look toward the abbey and hang his head as if he was being scolded. Then he slowly ambled back toward the ravine. His walk was like that of an animal, the stride different somehow than most Homo sapiens. Deedra experienced a stirring of sympathy for the poor creature. He could neither help his condition nor change it.

They couldn't see who was calling to him, but Deedra was certain it was Hannah. She seemed to have more control over the poor youth than Ricardo.

Not waiting for the sheriff, Deedra ran down the slope with the hope of getting a glimpse of the place where the mutant crossed to the abbey grounds. She was just in time to see him swinging across the ravine on a heavy rope. He landed on the other side. As he tied the rope to a tree limb, Hannah strode up to him, shaking her fist. She then hit him across the face with a stick.

Deedra stood behind a scrub tree and watched as Hannah shooed the poor thing toward the house. She couldn't hear what Hannah was saying, but the sound of her voice drifted across the arroyo. It was a raspy, scolding voice.

The sheriff arrived at her side, panting and demanding to know what she had seen.

"He has a heavy rope tied to that tree. He just swings across when he wants to get to this side. The rope is tied to a tree on the other side right now. But it is a way to get in or off the property," Deedra smiled as they walked to their cars. "Sheriff, it would be nice to know when that gadget is removed. You'll let me know, won't you?"

"Yes, I'll do that," Rex returned the smile, tipped his hat and drove off toward town.

Deedra slowly followed. Halfway there she changed her mind and drove to the old logging road where they had gone earlier, leaving her car parked in the abandoned forest camp. A thicket kept the car from being seen from even the third floor of the abbey. The road into the forest seemed in worse condition, though she reminded herself that the men had been with her at that time and it had not seemed quite so scary. Only their footprints told of their earlier visit. If someone else had passed that way they had left no sign of it.

At a place directly across from the front gates she hid behind a thatch of brambles and studied the abbey. It looked deserted and desolate. Its facade was dismal and grim, presenting a melancholy, haunted look.

Deedra circled around the front lawn, moving carefully from one hiding place to another until she reached the gate they had viewed from the helicopter.

The gate was unlocked. From there she could see Ricardo's lab, but the draperies were drawn. If Ricardo was in there no light indicated it. She cautiously moved from tree to shrub. She then waited to see if her movements had been noted. No sign of movement or sudden alertness from within the house indicated that she had been seen. At a place near the fence she viewed the back yard and then moved on to the faint trail leading down into the arroyo.

A light shone from the kitchen window. Her heart began thumping, her intuition telling her to get away from there. Ignoring the warning she waited. A light went on in an upper window. Hannah's silhouette appeared and the drapes were drawn, shutting Hannah from sight. It was a relief to know that Hannah was not outside anywhere.

Deedra scurried along the edge of the canyon until she reached the rock wall and found the place where the mutant had tied the rope. A noise caused her to turn. She stumbled and fell against a sticker shrub. Deedra remained unmoving for what seemed an eon of time. There was silence, no movement and no sudden opening of doors. Finally she began creeping along the rock wall going toward the road. It was when she reached the road that she realized she had lost the gun. It had probably fallen out of her jacket near that sticker shrub. She couldn't leave the gun there for Hannah or the mutant to find. Just the thought of that brought on a cold shudder. She retraced her steps back to the sticker shrub. Perspiration dripped from her whole body, causing her to feel quite damp by the time she found the gun. It was right where she had fallen. She leaned against the wall and breathed a prayer of thanks.

The back door suddenly opened. Ricardo emerged and began walking straight toward her.

She gripped the gun in her trembling hand.

When Ricardo reached a place near low-growing plants, he opened a door leading down into the cellar. As he descended, she glimpsed cement steps and walls. Then the door closed, cutting Ricardo off from view.

The door to the cellar was perfectly camouflaged. That meant that Ricardo didn't want anyone to know how to get into the underbelly of the abbey. Did it also mean that there wasn't an inside entry? That the passageways had indeed been boarded off?

She dared not follow. She simply waited for Ricardo to return. After a few tense minutes Ricardo opened the door, blinked as if the sudden daylight hurt his eyes and quickly strode to the house. He deliberately slammed the back door. Deedra heard his voice scolding and shouting. An answering voice sounded like Hannah replying in a more complacent tone. Deedra waited, thinking that Hannah would now emerge and go into the cellar, but she did not.

After a few indecisive minutes, and knowing that it was foolish even to think of going into the cellar alone, Deedra cautiously made her way to the cellar door. It suddenly creaked open.

She found herself staring into the beady eyes of the mutant who stood on the steps in front of her. He ignored her and ambled toward the kitchen muttering a sort of gibberish. He opened the back door without knocking and disappeared inside.

Ricardo appeared at a downstairs window and pulled the shade down. He hadn't looked toward the cellar entrance. If Ricardo had seen her standing there he gave no indication of it. He would have expected the cellar door to be open since the mutant had just emerged from it and entered the kitchen.

Still, Deedra just stood there. Fear kept her from going down the dank basement steps into the unknown labyrinth and whatever secrets were hidden there. Deedra knew the men wouldn't blame her if she just ran back to her car and drove away. But then she would always blame herself for avoiding the chance to help Sharlee, and perhaps even finding the missing Curt Ralston. Besides, hadn't Clete sent her up here to find out what was going on? She couldn't let Deke beat her out of that front-page story.

Slowly, Deedra went down the steps, pausing to listen for sounds of anything or anyone moving... anything alive. She felt in her jacket pockets to make certain the gun and flashlight were still there. Since the mutant was in the house, presumably to eat, she would make a fast tour, see if the missing Curt Ralston was there, and get out.

Suddenly the cellar door slammed shut and a bleak darkness surrounded her.

THIRTEEN

HANNAH'S VOICE COULD be heard through the closed cellar door. "Get out of my kitchen! You just stay down in them cellars! You've already caused us trouble! Go on now. And don't you come out until I tell you it's time to eat!"

She could hear the mutant crying. He sat on the steps and wept piteously. He didn't appear to notice Deedra who quickly ran up the steps past him and out the creaking door. If Hannah saw her, Deedra simply didn't care. She ran toward the rock wall, crashed through the foliage beside it and followed its length until she reached the road.

Once there she halted and glanced back toward the abbey. No one seemed to be in pursuit, but her heart still thumped heavily. Her breathing was shallow. She raced across the road, stumbling through the brambles until she reached the car. It was where she left it. For some reason she had expected to find it gone. Once inside the car she took a deep groaning breath of relief. The experience left her shaking, and worse, she had not accomplished what she had set out to do. Deedra felt slightly embarrassed that she had run away at the first sight of the mutant. She couldn't help feeling sorry for the poor creature, a slobbering, weeping, human wreck that was devastated by Hannah's scolding words.

Instead of going back to the newspaper, she drove to Sandy Harris' home, Land's End. Sandy was obviously just getting ready to go somewhere.

"Hi," she greeted. "Any news of Sharlee?"

Deedra shook her head. "I did see her at the window holding a child in her arms. At first I thought it was a large doll, but then it moved. I'm afraid it is as frail as Sharlee. I see that you are ready to go somewhere, so I'll make this brief. In the times you were up at the abbey, did you see a woman called Hannah, or a young giant of a teenager who is about seven feet tall?"

Sandy's eyes widened. "You're kidding!" she cried, "I would have mentioned it right away if I had seen either of them. I don't think Sharlee would have permitted another woman in her house in any event.

"And where would a big boy like that hide?"

"He obviously lives in the cellars. I know he's there because I left him a few minutes ago sitting on the cellar steps crying as if his heart would break. I understand that Ricardo Embustero is said to have a mentally-challenged son and the people in the town where he previously lived don't seem to know where the boy is or what happened to him. Do you think Ricardo could have brought the boy to the abbey?"

"I can't believe it! No one ever mentioned a boy, and I thought the cellars had been boarded up! I know that the one in the kitchen was because Sharlee and I watched the carpenters do it. The boards kept anyone from going down there, and anyone or anything from entering the house from those awful caverns under it. Ricardo didn't want the doors boarded up, but Sharlee insisted on it, really made a scene about it and Ricardo finally agreed."

"Ricardo did things Sharlee requested?"

"Yes. In those days anything Sharlee asked for, Ricardo granted. I thought then that he was really in love with her, sort of worshipped her, if you know what I mean. That was why when they finally moved into the abbey his sudden change of personality was so mysterious. He even developed that streak of white hair. It wasn't really very noticeable at first, but within a few weeks it was really striped. If I didn't know better, I'd think it wasn't the same Ricardo. I know that certain psychological trauma can change people's personalities...and quite suddenly. I gave that a lot of thought, did some reading on the subject. I decided that the old abbey must have played tricks on him. Maybe Ricardo encountered some poltergeist activities or allowed the atmosphere to unhinge his mind. He's very paranoid, you know. He was that way about his inventions even before they moved into the abbey. Always thought someone was trying to steal them. I just know that he seemed like a stranger to me after they moved from the summerhouse. In fact, when I went there, it was almost as if Ricardo didn't recognize me."

"Did Ricardo mention any relatives while you were still visiting Sharlee regularly?"

"No one in this part of the country. But I think he said there was a cousin who was also an inventor. I guess he wasn't as successful as Ricardo. He lived back East somewhere and Sharlee said he attended their wedding."

"You don't recall the cousin's name?"

Sandy's brows pulled together in a kind of frown.

"No, I don't remember being told his name, at least I don't recall it."

"I won't keep you any longer. Thanks for the information."

"Any time. Any news of Curt?"

"Afraid not," Deedra sighed. "I think the Ralston boy is hidden in the abbey cellars somewhere."

Sandy gasped. "A person could be hidden down there indefinitely!"

Deedra waited a moment, but Sandy didn't volunteer further comment. Deedra went to her car and Sandy disappeared within the house.

At the newspaper Deedra found Kortney busy at the computer. R.D. hadn't yet returned from the search for the missing boy.

Once again Deedra studied the files on Ricardo Embustero. There certainly were subtle changes, though Sandy could be right in saying he might have had some sort of psychological trauma. And there was always the possibility that Ricardo had been putting on an act for the public when Sharlee was in the spotlight. Perhaps Ricardo just reverted to his real self once they moved into the abbey where he could control things.

Feeling someone's gaze, Deedra looked up and was surprised to find Kortney staring at her.

"Kortney, have you ever seen Ricardo Embustero?"

Kortney blushed at having been caught staring. "Yes, he used to drive into town once or twice a week. He seemed very friendly then. I was surprised when Sandy Harris said he had refused to let her see Sharlee. Sandy was really hurt. She couldn't understand why Sharlee didn't contact her. They had been planning to make a movie together. I guess they had even discussed it with a movie producer. Trent Kettering. Sharlee was going to finance it. I have always thought Ricardo got wind of it, and didn't want Sharlee spending all that money. He is known to be… ah…very thrifty. I keep wondering if the old creep has been trying to get control of Sharlee's money.

Ricardo wouldn't be the first old lecher that has taken advantage of a rich woman. They say he's had several wives and that they were all rich, and now most of them are dead."

Deedra was surprised at Kortney's vehemence and knowledge of the people at the abbey. She had evidently spent time and thought on the situation. Deedra suspected that the people of Bermondy knew more than they let on, that they didn't tell strangers much about the people who lived here. And that Kortney was probably correct in her evaluation of Ricardo. Indeed, he'd had several rich wives, he did like money, and he did seem to have a cruel streak. Again, Deedra wondered if Ricardo had murdered any of those wives. And which wife was the mother of his mentally-challenged son?

SHE PLACED A CALL to Clete. "Have you learned anything further on Ricardo?"

After Clete had answered in the negative, she requested, "Check to see if there is any possibility that Ricardo might have murdered any of those former wives and find out how much money he actually inherited from them. Ricardo is also reported to have a cousin who is an inventor. I need the name of that cousin and where he is now. It would be interesting if he turns out to look like Ricardo."

"Hold on, Deedra. Where is all this leading?"

"Clete, I think Ricardo is trying to get control of Sharlee's money. There's evidence that Sharlee and the local doctor's wife had arranged to make a movie together. A woman named Sandy Harris. I don't know what name she used while modeling. She used to be featured in a popular shampoo commercial. Anyway, it appears that Sharlee was planning to finance the movie. Ricardo might not have liked that idea. I also think Curt Ralston is hidden in the cellars."

"So Ricardo is trying to prove that Sharlee is mentally unstable?"

"Yeah, I'm sure that's his plan."

When Deedra hung up, Kortney was looking at her with certain awe. "You really get things moving, don't you?"

Deedra smiled. "In my profession, Kortney, it's move or fall by the wayside. Then you never get any of the front-page bylines. You have to act tough and try to give the impression that you know more than you do."

Kortney nodded, though Deedra wasn't sure Kortney understood. She had already turned her attention back to the computer.

Deedra went back to reading the files on Ricardo, Sharlee, the doctor, and with more careful and curious interest, the banker.

The men returned with no news of the missing boy.

"Have a cup of coffee, then I have a tale to tell,"

Deedra stated. After they were seated, she told them of her afternoon adventures. "So there's a cellar entrance in the back yard, but Sandy Harris told me they had boarded up the entranceway in the kitchen. Of course, Ricardo could have opened it up again, though it doesn't seem likely since they use that outside entrance."

"That still doesn't make sense for them to harm Curt," R.D. remarked.

"Somehow they found out Curt had received a note for help from Sharlee and then they caught him snooping around the place," Deedra replied.

"Even so, it doesn't make sense to harm the boy. After all, the sheriff has been up there asking questions even though no charges have been made. It would be dangerous, and kind of stupid, to harm the boy," Deke said.

Deedra sighed. Deke was right, of course. But he hadn't seen Hannah or Ricardo up close and personal and lots of things about that odd couple didn't make sense. Sharlee's self-imposed reclusive actions didn't make sense.

R.D. spoke up. "I did learn that Hannah shops in that town to the north. She is something of a curiosity there. She always pays in cash. No one seems to know exactly where she lives. She doesn't carry on unnecessary conversations. I hear she puts people off when they ask questions."

"Well, there's nothing illegal about that. Just strange that Hannah doesn't shop in Bermondy, but then again perhaps people here have put her off. She isn't pretty and she knows it. Her manner of dress causes amusement. It's my guess that they haven't wanted anyone to know she is a permanent resident at the abbey," Nick suggested.

"I suspect," Deedra remarked, "that Hannah out in the daylight and away from the abbey does cause a certain amusement, but up at the abbey she is just plain spooky. Have the authorities sent out an all-points bulletin on Curt?"

"They did the other day. Absolutely no responses," R.D replied.

"The only place left to search besides dragging the lake is the depths of that ravine." Deke said in a glum voice.

"Yeah, well, the sheriff has been on the lookout for vultures. They would have gathered by this time if there was a hurt or dead body down there," R.D. reminded them.

With that they called it a day. Deke, Nick, and Deedra went off to dinner at the Bermondy Inn. Afterwards she and Deke went to a movie at the local theater. It was one they had both wanted to see, but hadn't yet found the opportunity.

Once again Deke spent the night on Deedra's couch, though they had a slightly romantic interlude earlier. She cursed herself as a fool in allowing Deke to take over her emotions. But love was like that, and she didn't seem able to do anything about it. Deedra hadn't found anyone who intrigued her like Deke did. She vaguely wondered if Daryl Walters was the only offer of marriage she would ever have.

The next day dawned with Deedra's determination to search the foliage around the old pond and summerhouse on the abbey grounds. Curt could be hidden there for quite some time. He might even have drowned in that stagnant pond or could have had an accident while snooping around. Ricardo or Hannah might not have deliberately hurt him. Though the sight of scary old Hannah carrying that shovel kept recurring to Deedra. What kind of digging had Hannah been doing with that shovel?

While the men went to find out where the search would take them that day, Deedra drove out the old logging road where she forced herself to get out of the car and retrace her tracks to the abandoned forest camp. She was trembling despite the heat of the day. She took a long look at the old abbey and sighed. She left her jacket along with the gun and flashlight in the car. If she was caught trespassing, there wasn't much Ricardo could do about it. But if she was carrying a gun he could bring charges against her. Since Deedra didn't intend to enter the house or cellars she didn't want to chance losing the gun again. Also the gun and flashlight were cumbersome.

This time Deedra walked alongside the road opposite the abbey. She then crossed over near the bridge, arriving on the far side of the rock wall. Instead of entering the grounds by the front gates, she scurried along the rock wall until she found a place where some of the stones had fallen away. She used them as hand and foot holds to scale the wall. It wasn't a difficult feat. Before dropping to the ground she carefully surveyed the area. The mutant didn't seem to be roaming about. She didn't see Hannah either. Satisfied, she dropped to the ground finding herself near the path to the old pond. She waited a few moments before going on, listening for sounds and getting her exact location in mind. She wanted to make certain which way to go in case someone was lurking in the heavy foliage. She cautiously made her way to the pond. It was the first place she wanted to look. She was half-expecting to find Curt's body floating in its slimy water. But the pond did not appear disturbed. The water was about four feet deep and a body would eventually surface.

With a broken branch she poked and prodded in the water, but only managed to raise a fetid stink. A side path led to an area she hadn't seen on her earlier visit. She looked under every thick thatch of foliage, carefully moving aside brambles and branches, on the lookout for places that showed recent digging.

She perspired with the heat of the day and the oppressiveness of moss and moldering leaves. The dank odor of decay smote her nostrils. A shudder sent a chill across her perspiring body. Get on with it, she chided, and moved through another bramble patch. After inspecting the area she found herself near the summerhouse. It was something of a relief to leave the thickets of rank foliage and walk in the shade of the old oak trees. Heavy vines clutched the oak branches and dangled to the ground. They writhed across the pathway in thick ropes like reptiles, giving Deedra a crawly sensation, her memory conjuring up the rattle of snakes. She shuddered. The vines didn't look trampled. There was no indication that anyone had traversed that way for several days, if not weeks. She circled the summerhouse until she reached a place where she could see the turret windows. Sharlee was standing in the window again, the child cradled in her arms. She didn't see Deedra. Deedra knew that if Sharlee had seen her, she would not react for fear of alerting Ricardo to her presence.

Deedra went down the summerhouse steps, moved the vines away from the door and strangely, found the door unlocked. She found it odd that the door didn't squeak when she opened it. Only thin light filtered through the lecherous vines that covered the windows. It was evident that the place had once been used as living quarters, though now only old dishes reposed on the shelves. Broken chairs were placed beside the table. Old cookware still rested on a large wood range. She suspected that Ricardo had put the mutant out here and it hadn't proved workable. Evidently this wasn't the place where Sharlee and Trent held their romantic rendezvous. This place was not even remotely romantic. A moldering smell pervaded the rooms, the damp stickiness giving off an uncomfortable miasma. Spider webs created a filmy lace that looped from the corner to an overhead beam where a large black spider had taken up residence.

She didn't disturb the web. No sense leaving evidence of her visit. After looking around, she determined Curt Ralston was not there. When she left, Deedra replaced the vine across the door.

Always on the lookout for Hannah, she kept moving through the foliage, eventually arriving at the place where the rock wall ended. It was where the ravine dropped off into space. After a glance at the back yard, she began to retrace her steps along the rock wall and passed several old oaks with those trailing snake-like vines. They clutched the trees with strangulating holds. Leaves riffled in the wind as if moved by ghostly hands. It was an eerie place, a gothic setting if she ever saw one. It was easy to imagine that ghosts and ghouls roamed about the old abbey and its grounds. The unrestrained growth of plants and vines only added to its haunted mien. She neared the pond again, and when she rounded a large oak, she met Hannah standing in the path, blocking her way.

"Oh, Miss Hannah! You certainly gave me a fright. I know you didn't give me permission, but Mr. Embustero did the other day. I just wanted to return and see if the missing Ralston boy could have wandered onto your property, and met with some kind of accident. I thought he might have fallen into the pond and drowned."

Hannah frowned as if she had trouble comprehending what Deedra had said. "Who did you say was missing?"

"Curt Ralston, the boy who delivered newspapers to you here." Why was Hannah pretending ignorance since Deedra knew that the F.B.I. men had made inquiries?

"Why did you think he might be here?" Hannah gestured to the grounds.

"Well, you know how young boys are. They like to explore. I supposed he might have wanted to see what was here. I thought he might have fallen into the pond or perhaps fell off the wall and broke his leg."

Hannah stared at her, uncertain how to answer.

"I'm sure if the boy had been here, I would have found him. I go through these grounds almost every day. It's a relief to get out of the house. Taking care of Sharlee is very demanding. I'll walk you to the front gates."

Deedra was more than glad to have her do just that, silently giving thanks that she had been wise enough to leave the gun in the car.

"Where are you parked?" Hannah asked when they passed through the front gates.

"I'm over there in that abandoned forest camp. I looked all around there for signs of the boy, and eventually I ended up here. I recalled seeing that old pond, and thought I'd better have a look-see. It seems that almost every place around Bermondy has been searched. There isn't a clue as to what happened to that delivery boy."

"Perhaps he was kidnapped?" Hannah suggested.

"They haven't received a ransom note if he has been," Deedra replied.

"You can assure the sheriff that the boy isn't here," she commanded.

Deedra nodded and scurried across the road into the thickets, knowing Hannah couldn't see her once she got several leagues away. She huddled behind a scrub tree and looked back. What would the old woman do now? Deedra did wish Hannah would learn to wash her body with a deodorant soap. An odd musty smell clung to Hannah, an odor that was reminiscent of the dungeons under the house or of mice in a dirty corner.

Sharlee was standing at the upstairs window watching Hannah. When Hannah turned back toward the abbey, Sharlee vanished.

As she walked to her car, Deedra pondered the fact that Hannah had seemed genuinely puzzled that the Ralston boy was missing. Had Hannah thought the F.B.I. men's visit was about the mutant youth? Had Ricardo misled Hannah about the reason for the F.B.I. men's visit? Something told Deedra that Hannah has just learned information that she had been unaware of, that she hadn't known the missing boy was the one who had delivered newspapers to the abbey.

FOURTEEN

CLETE CALLED to find out the latest news on the missing boy. Deedra dictated a story to him for the evening edition. Afterwards, Clete said, "Deedra, I don't want you going up to the abbey alone again. You have enough info for a couple of features, anyway. You can tie Curt Ralston in with Sharlee later."

"Did you get the info I wanted?" Deedra challenged.

"The cousin's name is Carlo Embustero. I'm trying to get a photo now. We're doing a background check, but rumor has it that Carlo has vamoosed."

"Oh, oh!"

"Yeah. Maybe Carlo's taken on a new identity. If so, what's happened to the real Ricardo?"

"That," Deedra exclaimed, "would explain Sharlee's mental confusion. Ricardo not seeming to be Ricardo; Sharlee being unable to shake that idea. Maybe she was told that she was just imagining things, that she wasn't well. It would establish that precept in her mind. And in that environment it could easily take root."

"Just watch yourself, Deedra. If what we suspect

is true, then you're probably dealing with a murderer. And you know murderers aren't afraid to kill again if they think it's necessary to protect themselves. You go wandering around up there and you could vanish just like the Ralston boy."

Clete tried to get Deedra to promise that she wouldn't go there alone. But she didn't. She simply agreed with him that it would be dangerous.

The men returned after dark, plainly discouraged and glum. The search had officially been called off.

"There's no sign of the boy," Nick said. "It's as if he's been taken to another planet."

"Or into a deep dark cavern," Deedra muttered.

Both men chose to ignore her remark.

R.D. entered and said, "I think every home and basement in town has been searched. Curt's father collapsed, and is in the hospital with his wife. It's almost a relief to get him away from the search efforts. It's difficult to cope with that kind of grief."

"It's damn funny we haven't discovered even a shred of Curt's clothing. I thought we would after finding the bicycle," Nick muttered.

"Curt wouldn't go anywhere without his bike. He wanted a new one, but he wouldn't have just walked off and left that one," R.D. remarked.

"You know," Nick suggested, "whoever took Curt disposed of the bicycle because it was safer to do so, and why wasn't it discovered sooner with everyone looking for it? It wasn't really hidden. It was as if someone put it there a day or two after Curt disappeared. Why? It's easier to hide a body than to hide a bicycle. Now that means that someone in a car transported it there, though no one saw anyone do that the afternoon Curt vanished. And we know from Mrs. Seltzer's testimony that Curt rode his bike back toward town after delivering her newspaper. Whatever happened to Curt happened right after he left Mrs. Seltzer."

During dinner at the Bermondy Inn, Deke muttered something about the day passing without making any progress. Deedra took that opportunity to announce her information.

"That's not exactly true, Deke," she said. Deedra then told them about Ricardo's cousin, Carlo.

"That puts a whole new perspective on this thing. Perhaps this is a murder case, after all. And Sharlee knows or at least suspects she's living in a house with the man who has killed her husband," Nick said. "That's bound to have traumatic results."

"The point is," Deke reminded, "did Curt pose a threat to the Embusteros? Did Curt know something that would endanger them? It still doesn't make sense for them to have kidnapped him and taken the chance that there would be an intensive investigation."

"I learned something else," Nick told them. "It's about Sandy Harris. Sandy was once engaged to Trent

Kettering, the alleged father of Sharlee's child. Of course, that was before Sharlee met Trent, but we can't be certain Sandy told Sharlee about it. The good doctor's wife was Sandy North in her modeling career days. Her real name is Sandra Northrup. She was born in Boston and started her modeling career in New York. She was featured on the covers of several magazines in the late '90s. Shortly after she stopped seeing Trent Kettering she married Dr. Harris."

"Wow!" Deedra muttered.

"The more we look into this, the more complicated it gets." Deke ran a hand through his hair. There were circles under his eyes and Deedra suspected they were not caused by exertion in looking through brambles all day.

Nick continued. "I have another bit of information. Hannah is Ricardo's first wife, not his sister."

"Now," Deedra challenged, "why would Ricardo want an ex-wife around?"

Nick shrugged. "She's the only living ex-wife. Maybe she has something on Ricardo, maybe she's the mutant's mother."

"That would make sense. That poor creature was broken-hearted when Hannah scolded him like that. Hannah is the one who seems to be able to control him," Deedra replied.

The men stared at her in surprise. Then she realized that she hadn't told them of her adventures.

"Getting back to Hannah," Nick threw Deedra a dark look, "she seems to have up and moved away from her town of residence without a word to anyone. One day Hannah just left without leaving a forwarding address. It was about the same time that Ricardo ordered Sandy Harris off the abbey property."

Deedra and Deke exchanged glances.

"That," Deedra reminded, "would be why Sandy never saw or heard of Hannah."

"We checked Hannah out, learned that she received some sort of monthly pension, though she is too young for Social Security."

"Ricardo's alimony?"

"Yes, we thought that was it," Nick replied.

"Nick, I don't mean to pry, but how many men do you have working for you?" Deedra challenged.

"Who said they were men, Deedra?" Nick countered.

She laughed to cover the reprimand.

"Ricardo must have had some contact with Hannah or she wouldn't have known where he was," Deke muttered.

"You forget all the publicity at the time Ricardo and Sharlee got married. If he and Hannah were never divorced, then Sharlee really isn't his wife," Nick reminded.

Deke looked shocked.

Deedra shook her head, wondering why anything

shocked Deke. Deke's emotions were confused by this investigation. Though she sympathized with him, at the same time she was miffed about it. Why did Deke expend emotional energy on something that had nothing to do with him now?

"Since the mutant boy wasn't around when Sharlee married Ricardo…ah…when she thought she married Ricardo, then he must have arrived with Hannah. Hannah evidently knew where he was all those years. Perhaps she cared for the boy, though Hannah could scarcely have kept him hidden in the small house she resided in. He was probably in some institution somewhere, and then got too big and too old for them to manage. He might even be older than eighteen and that would force him out into the world again." Nick's people had certainly looked into Hannah's background.

"The thing is," Deedra reminded, "did Ricardo send for Hannah, or did Hannah just pack up and go to the abbey?"

"My operator thinks Hannah was told by whatever facility cared for the mutant that they could no longer manage him and she was forced to move in on Ricardo, or at least leave the boy with him."

"Then if Carlo arrived and took over Ricardo's identity, did it mean he accompanied Hannah here? Someone had to help bring that boy to the abbey. Suppose Hannah got Carlo to help her and they planned to put the squeeze on Ricardo, and Ricardo objected? They could have killed Ricardo and put his body down in the cellars. That would leave Carlo free to take on Ricardo's identity, money, Sharlee, and everything else," Deedra suggested.

"That makes sense, though the missing boy still does not fit into that scheme of things," Deke reminded.

"What if," Deedra suggested, "Curt went up there and ran into the mutant. What if the mutant dragged him off to the cellars and Ricardo and Hannah didn't learn of it until it was too late?"

Nick sat up straighter. "You could be right," he said. "It would certainly explain why your informing her of the missing delivery boy seemed to surprise Hannah. She might not have known yet that Curt Ralston was in the cellars. And she might not have told Ricardo...ah...Carlo, fearing some kind of reprisal."

"The real reason they are so hesitant to have visitors is because Carlo has assumed Ricardo's identity and they can't let anyone suspect or learn of it. Sharlee's having a baby was just the thing they needed to divert the sheriff's suspicions. Everyone knows that sometimes women suffer from post-partem depression. It's easy to explain why a woman would be depressed and frail-looking."

"But we can't prove all this," Deke said. "We have

to be able to get Sharlee and the baby out of there before they really send her over the brink!"

"There's nothing now that we can get a warrant on. Suspicions aren't reasonable cause. You have to have some kind of evidence," Nick muttered.

"And that evidence is probably down in those dark cellars along with the spiders and the mutant," Deke muttered.

The next morning they all drove out to the abbey where Deke took several photos.

"How the heck did you get the courage to go wandering about here, Deedra?" Deke asked.

"Part of my job. Deke, you know I don't get those front-page stories just sitting around and letting them happen," she replied.

"Didn't the fact that the abbey is supposed to be haunted, and Chuck Preston telling you about those holographic image tricks frighten you?" Deke challenged.

"Of course. That is one damn spooky place, but something has to be done for Sharlee and that baby. And if old Ricardo has actually been murdered, then we have to find that out."

Though they had hoped to see Sharlee at an upstairs window, she didn't appear. They left without getting a glimpse of her. It was a disappointment to all of them.

Kortney was on the phone when they walked into

the newspaper office. "Here she is now," she said as she handed the phone to Deedra.

"Ricardo does have a cousin named Carlo," Clete told her, "and they do look very much alike. He moved about the same time as Hannah did, and he does have a white streak of hair down the middle of his head." Deedra did not tell Clete that Nick had already learned of these facts.

After she hung up she asked R.D. "When did the first rumor about the mutant, giant, whatever, start?"

"Let's see. It was a young couple parked out near that narrow bridge. Everyone thought someone had just played a trick on them. But let me tell you, they were really frightened. I talked to the young man later and he said he'd never go there at night again."

"That stopped the rumors?"

"No. About a month later, another young couple walking along that road reported seeing a 'giant man' up near the bridge. They didn't go any further. After that, most of the young people avoided the area for their…ah…romantic adventures. Then we started getting complaints from the youngsters delivering the newspapers out there. Most of the time they just wanted to leave the papers at the entrance gates."

"Then you hired the Ralston boy?"

"Yes, though I learned later that he had applied for that route on a dare from a boy who previously had it. That boy told Curt the house was really haunted. That it was too spooky to go out there. Evidently Curt assured him that there were no such things as ghosts and spooks. Then the boy dared Curt to take that delivery route and see for himself."

Now Deedra understood R.D.'s sense of guilt in sending Curt on that route.

"If you ask Curt's friends what they think happened to him, they'd tell you he's out at the abbey somewhere. They all think old Ricardo kidnapped him," R.D. said.

Nick and Deedra exchanged glances.

"Did," Deedra challenged, "any of the other boys say anything about Curt seeing strange things going on there?"

"Well, when he first disappeared, there were comments like 'Big Foot's got him', remarks like that. Now they are just quiet, and scared, and mostly don't say anything. I have to drive out there with the newspaper myself. I can't take a chance sending another child there."

Obviously R.D. believed that Curt Ralston had met his fate near or in the abbey. She guessed if she talked to the townspeople, there would be a consensus of that opinion.

The sheriff walked in and they were duty bound to inform him about the things they had learned. "Yes," Rex said, "I just got word from the local authorities about Hannah Embustero. I didn't know about Carlo, however."

"My editor is faxing a photo. It should be here any minute," Deedra told him.

It had just arrived and R.D. handed it to the sheriff.

"I'll be damned," Rex Walling muttered. "It's the perfect image of Ricardo. If that's really Carlo," he added.

"Do you have sufficient cause to get a warrant now?" Deedra asked.

"I'm certainly going to try." The sheriff nodded his thanks to her, and strode out.

"My, he's a handsome man. Is he married?" she asked R.D.

"Nope. Lots of young women in this town would like to be the object of Rex Walling's attentions. I understand he has a steady girl over at the coast somewhere. I know he goes over there whenever he has a day off."

"Tough," she muttered, and noted Deke's frown.

Deedra turned her smile on R.D.

"A girl like me keeps trying to meet eligible men. I have marriage in mind and want a family. Isn't that the American woman's dream?"

R.D. nodded and blushed suddenly, taking an interest in the papers on his desk.

Nick threw Deke a lopsided grin.

Deke stared at Deedra, a frown causing his eyebrows to nearly join together, his eyes to shoot sparks. "Later," he muttered.

FIFTEEN

AFTER PHONING CLETE the next morning, Deedra drove toward the abbey. She parked her car in a glen several leagues away from the old bridge. She walked from the road down to the edge of the ravine and followed along side of it, examining each thicket and bramble. She was looking for strands of clothing, something the men might have missed in their hurried search for a body or bicycle. If the mutant crossed over on the rope he might have wandered into this area and perhaps had caught Curt there.

She stayed in the shelter of the foliage, not wanting either Ricardo or Hannah to see her. Perhaps they wouldn't be watching since the men had completed their search.

Deedra reached the place where the giant youth had swung across the ravine on the rope. There was a faint trail leading down and across the landslide. It led to the far edge just below the back of the abbey grounds. She had located another exit should the need arise. She knew now that she was going into the abbey; that she was going to try and rescue Sharlee. Although she didn't know how that could be accomplished. There didn't seem to be any other way to resolve the situation. The law couldn't move on it without probable cause, and Sharlee was obviously helpless to do anything to help herself.

After a deep breath and a muttered prayer, she started down the trail toward the landslide. Rubble skittered in rivulets ahead of her. The path angled over the landslide. It was dangerous there. Her feet were sinking into the unstable dirt and gravel. She was halfway across the landslide when she noted Hannah standing at the edge of the ravine. Fortunately she was looking the other way and hadn't yet seen Deedra. She held perfectly still, not daring to move a muscle.

And Hannah moved away without seeing her. Still, Deedra didn't move until Hannah disappeared from her sight. She breathed a sigh of relief and continued on, though all of her being urged her to go back to her car, to get away from that place, to forget the old abbey and its spooky inhabitants. Only Deedra's sense of duty and the plight of Sharlee and her baby, and perhaps that of Curt Ralston, kept her moving forward.

The trail was more precarious than it had looked from topside. Several times, rubble threatened to send her down the steep sides. By the time she reached the edge of the abbey grounds she was panting with exhaustion.

She peered into the grounds from behind the

foliage, trying to see if Hannah was still about. There was no movement at the back of the house. No one seemed to be moving in the kitchen area. There were no sounds, a condition that made it seem even more eerie. What a crotchety old place this was, manifesting its reputation even by its silence.

Deedra shook her head to rid the imaginative thoughts and scuttled toward the cellar entrance. She was about to open it when the door flew open and she was eyeball to eyeball with the mutant. His eyes were very red and dark circles hung beneath his lower lids. A feral look gleamed from them.

The mutant emitted a snorting noise of surprise.

Deedra panicked. She smothered a scream that would have alerted Ricardo and Hannah. For a century-long time they simply stared at each other.

Then in an unexpected movement, the mutant gathered her under his arm and quickly re-entered the cellar, clattering down the cement steps. He carried her effortlessly. When she wriggled, he clasped her closer to him. She dared not struggle, fearing that he might crush her to death, even though he carried her loosely and only tightened his grip when Deedra struggled.

She saw that the stairwell walls were covered in dark lichen and moss. They entered a large cavern illuminated by a light from the filthy windows under Ricardo's lab. Close to the walls, spider webs festooned from ceiling to floor. The smell of carrion hung in the air, causing bile to rise in her mouth.

A new spurt of fear shot through her at the sight of a large skeleton stretched out on a trundle bed. It was completely covered with spider webs.

The mutant went to the bed and stared down at the skeleton, tears filling his bleary eyes. "Da," he mumbled. He pushed aside some of the spider webs with his free hand and patted the skeleton affectionately causing the bones to creak. "Da," he gurgled again, and emitted what seemed like a groan of grief.

A shudder overtook Deedra, causing the mutant to hold her tighter.

They passed into a dank cavern with earthen walls, though the floor had been cemented. Damp and slimy lichens covered the sides giving off a musty fetidness and the impression that secret crawly things squirmed in it. The smell of something dead clung to the semi-darkness. Not detouring the mutant plowed ahead into other caverns dimly lighted through windows at the base of the abbey.

Deedra experienced a sense of being caught up in someone else's nightmare, carried by a crazed mutant through funereal cellar-like rooms. The feeling of reality hit her when she realized that only great courage or luck would allow her to escape.

A rat scurried across the cement floor in front of

them. The giant youth stomped it to death, uttering sounds of pure hatred with each stomp.

Deedra fought down nausea and succeeded in controlling another shudder. Until that moment she hadn't experienced such terrorizing fear. It was all consuming and was accompanied by desperation... and a sense of helplessness.

The giant youth carried her through a series of empty caverns. In places there were stacks of old newspapers and clothing. One cavern contained empty wine racks. At last they reached a room near the end of the labyrinth where the creature threw Deedra onto an old couch whose springs had long since escaped the captivity of its cushions. Faint light filtered through two windows and Deedra realized this cavern room was under the rooms at the very front of the abbey. A rough-planked table laden with several thick candles stood in the center of the room along with a heavy old-fashioned rocking chair. Litter was piled in one corner and there was no sign of food. With its rat population it was not surprising.

The mutant lit one of the candles.

In another corner was what she had thought was a heap of rags. When the creature tenderly picked it up, Curt Ralston's head lolled lifelessly to one side.

Deedra screamed.

Obviously Curt had been dead for several days.

Deedra cried as she watched the young giant rock

the dead boy, tears streaming own his puffy face, real grief shining from his reddish eyes. She took advantage of his preoccupation and moved toward the door. He immediately threw the body into the corner, and grasped her arm in a tight grip that hurt her. When she went back toward the couch, he released his hold and mumbled. He jabbered as if trying to communicate with her. He looked toward the entrance and then at her, shook his head and muttered something that sounded like, "No, no."

He picked up the dead boy's body again and rocked and crooned over it until Deedra thought she couldn't tolerate the sight and sound of it another minute.

Nausea choked off her screams. She tried to force herself to think, to turn her mind away from the mutant's actions. Had he accidentally killed Curt, and was that why he wept and crooned over the body? Had Ricardo or Hannah put Curt down here to prevent his escaping and then the giant youth, looking for companionship, unwittingly crushed him to death, not aware of his own strength? If Curt had struggled to get away, the mutant could easily have broken his neck or back.

Though Deedra didn't think it possible, her fear deepened into the very marrow of her bones, leaving her strangely weak.

The cause of Curt's disappearance was suddenly clear. Curt had been caught on the abbey grounds and the giant had secreted him in the cellars. Hannah and Ricardo probably hadn't been aware of that fact until the sheriff or F.B.I. men came looking for him. If they had caught Curt, they would have sent him on his way after scaring him enough so that he wouldn't return. The Embusteros would be quite aware that a child's disappearance aroused community action as nothing else did. A search of the abbey would have been disastrous. Now she knew it was the mutant, in his loneliness and misery who had inadvertently caused Curt's death.

His crooning and mutterings echoed around the dank catacombs causing Deedra to wonder if they could hear him upstairs.

Shudders of revulsion swept over her as the youth cuddled and caressed Curt Ralston. Curt's body was rapidly deteriorating, the stench wafting a nauseous miasma.

Was the skeleton that the mutant called "Da," that of Ricardo? And was that why the mutant hadn't taken her to Ricardo or Hannah right away? If he was afraid of them, she might have a chance to talk her way out of these awful caverns. The youth, who had been watching her closely, seemed to understand what was said to him. He simply couldn't talk, and Deedra knew better than to let him know that she was afraid of him. Nevertheless, the way he gently cuddled and crooned over Curt's body caused her a certain sympathy. How terrible for this unfortunate person to be so lonely, so unloved and to have nothing to love, no one he could talk to…to have nothing.

She noted a trap door in the ceiling right over the table. From their location in the cellars, she guessed it opened into the upstairs hallway near the stairs to the turret rooms. Could she get into the house that way? The mutant would never be able to get his huge body through the opening so perhaps the Embusteros hadn't thought it necessary to board it up. The problem was whether the mutant would let her. No matter what, she dared not rouse his anger.

Deedra glanced at the youth. He shook his head at her as if he had somehow guessed her thoughts and hugged Curt's body closer. Did the mutant realize that he was going to have to give up the boy…and soon? The thought of the skeleton flashed through her mind. Could it really be Ricardo Embustero, and if so why had it been placed in the cellars? Was it here to prevent discovery or make it look as if the mutant was guilty?

The grotesqueness of her situation was mind shattering. Deedra realized that she would have to fight to keep her mind from slipping off into uncharted areas of thought and emotion. She knew that if she were kept down in these caverns for an indefinite period of time, she would surely be affected both psychologically and physically. Would Deke and Nick ever find out what happened to her? They would find her car and perhaps begin to trace her footsteps, though she doubted they would think she had crossed the ravine over that landslide. They were more likely to think she had gone directly in through the front gates and met an uncertain fate within the abbey. But the search wouldn't begin for several hours yet and it would be twenty-four hours before the law would start its own search.

The thought of spending twenty-four hours with this dead body-cuddling youth was really grossing her out.

SIXTEEN

THE DAMPNESS OF the cavern began to seep into Deedra's bones. It had been a hot day and she hadn't worn a jacket. The very thought of being chilled by hours of captivity filled her with an icy dread...that and the fact that she might never, ever, leave these cold dungeons.

Hours passed. Hours in which Deedra saw large rats scurry about, a thing that caused the mutant instant rage. He stomped to death any that passed near him. He was incensed when one ran up his leg and began eating on the flesh of Curt Ralston's arm. The mutant crushed the rat in his hands, the rat's innards bulging through the fur.

Deedra gagged and vomited.

The rats scurried to the vomit, and in a few moments there was no sign of it. She screamed at them, kicked at them, but nothing seemed to deter them. They scuttled about looking for more morsels.

The youth was obviously upset and finally took the boy's body into the cavern where the skeleton had been laid out. What thoughts ran through the poor creature's mind? Why hadn't he tried to leave the abbey and its inhabitants?

A moment after he left the room, Deedra climbed onto the table under the trap door and tried to push it open. At last it moved, but the mutant suddenly reappeared and threw her onto the floor. For a moment, Deedra thought her leg was broken. She lay on the floor and groaned, allowing the pain to take over. She rubbed her leg for several minutes, minutes in which the mutant seemed fascinated by her. His beady eyes gleamed, and he emitted guttural sounds from somewhere deep in his body.

At last Deedra was able to crawl to the broken chair. It was a straight-backed chair that she hoped to use later to stand on while attempting to climb through the trap door.

The mutant uttered warning sounds at her. It was as if he was scolding her like Hannah had scolded him. After an eternity of time, he lapsed into a half-sleep. Deedra was still cautious because he occasionally opened an eye to see where she was and what she was doing.

Time dragged on and on, time in which she allowed her thoughts to escape to other scenes. She simply couldn't dwell on her terrible predicament. In reverting to other times, to other places, envisioning scenes from her childhood, she maintained her sanity. Then she would flit back to the present with a jerk. She prayed, wondering what Deke and Nick were doing, if anything, to find her.

Hours later the giant youth began snoring. At first it was only snuffling, then ear-splitting wheezes that gurgled and whistled.

Slowly and cautiously, she stood up. She waited a moment to make certain the mutant wouldn't suddenly knock her to the floor again. But the snores continued. Carefully, she placed the chair on the table and climbed onto it. Again she waited.

The mutant snored on.

She climbed onto the chair.

The mutant's breathing changed. He moved and changed position.

She froze, fear seeming to cut off her breathing.

He groaned and muttered, threw his hands about as if having a nightmare. Then, after a time, began that awful crooning as if he was cuddling the boy in his sleep. Finally, the snoring began again.

She pushed the trap door open. It squeaked slightly, but didn't wake the mutant. Despite her bruised leg, she quickly hoisted herself up through the trap door, finding herself in the dark hallway near the turret stairs. After a quick glance around, she carefully replaced the trap door and crept into the heavy shadows where she melded into the night. After waiting to see if there was movement or noise, she crept up the turret stairs. Halfway up, Deedra heard the sound of footsteps and huddled in the shadow of the railing.

It was Hannah marching toward the front door.

Deedra scuttled up the turret stairs and hid behind the heavy draperies of a window on the landing. She wasn't any too soon for Hannah strode up the stairs in her clomping way and went into Sharlee's room.

In a few moments Deedra heard the sound of voices.

A soft noise on the stairs alerted her to the fact that Ricardo/Carlo stood several steps away from her hiding place. He was listening to Hannah and Sharlee. He scarcely moved, his manner that of an animal ready to scurry for safety at the first noise or movement. Did he not trust Hannah?

The sounds of Hannah's heavy tread sent Ricardo/Carlo tiptoeing down the stairs and up the hall where he vanished into the shadows.

Hannah appeared flustered, disturbed about something, and rubbed her hands together in a fretful manner. Had Sharlee refused to do something, resisted Hannah in some way? There was no doubt that Hannah was upset and before she disappeared down the hall she sent a resentful look up the turret stairs.

When Hannah disappeared, Deedra drew a breath of relief. She had scarcely breathed while Hannah was near. The old woman seemed to sense when something was awry. Just having escaped the cellar was trauma enough without having a run-in with Hannah.

Deedra waited a few minutes just in case Hannah decided to return, then crept into Sharlee's rooms. Sharlee wasn't in the first of the rooms that contained shelves of books, a small television and comfortable furniture. A cough alerted her to Sharlee's location in a small room near the front windows.

Just in time Deedra remembered the room was monitored on the surveillance system. She waited until Sharlee turned her way and then beckoned her into the other room.

Though Sharlee was surprised, shocked actually, she didn't give it away, proving her expertise as an actress. If Ricardo/Carlo had been watching on the monitor, he wouldn't have learned of Deedra's presence from Sharlee.

Once in the other room, Sharlee whispered, "How did you get in here?"

"Never mind how. How can I get you out?"

"I don't know. I've tried everything. You know how he has the house on a surveillance system?" Sharlee whispered.

Deedra nodded. "Does Hannah leave the back door unlocked?"

"Most of the time so that Tito can get in without breaking down the door."

"Who is Tito?"

"Ricardo's son. Ricardo thought he could bring the boy into normal intelligence and tried various experiments on him. Nothing worked. The boy just grew into that enormous size, and lost the ability to talk."

"How did Ricardo expect to do that?"

"By changing the boy's brain chemistry. Ricardo fully believed he could do it. He didn't know anything about DNA coding or he might even have tried gene splicing."

"Did you know that Tito has the delivery boy's body in the cellars? I think he killed him, crushed him to death."

Sharlee gasped, her hand covering her mouth to stifle the scream, additional fear filling her eyes. This news made Sharlee even more fearful for her baby.

"You have a baby?" When Sharlee nodded, "How old is he?"

"He's almost a year now. He wants to go outside, and he should be allowed to, but Hannah and Ricardo always prevent that. I'm afraid for the baby. No telling what Ricardo is planning to do. He has changed so much in the past few months, it's almost as if he's a completely different person from the man I married. I just don't understand it all."

"Didn't you go to the hospital to have the baby?

Surely Ricardo would want the best for you and his child?"

"He isn't Ricardo's child, he's Trent Kettering's son. Ricardo is impotent so he knew the child couldn't be his. When he learned that I was pregnant he locked me up for months and months. I had the baby here and Hannah delivered it."

"You don't even have a birth certificate for the baby?" Deedra experienced shock. No birth certificate, no baby. Ricardo/Carlo could do what he wanted with the child. There would be no evidence that there had ever been a child. He could simply say that Sharlee carried a large doll around; that she had only imagined that it was a baby.

"We have to figure a way to get out of here. It's already getting dark, so we can't leave tonight. I have friends who are probably looking for me right now. They will check here since they know I'm trying to find a way to get you out of here. In the meantime, we need to plan a way of escaping. Once we get outside the abbey we can get away."

"How though? Ricardo has the room where I keep the baby under surveillance and the room near the windows is monitored. At night he has a siren thing attached to the front and back doors, so that anyone going in or out sets it off. I tried to leave that way one night, so I know. The siren is enough to scare anyone to death. It woke the baby, and he didn't stop crying for a long time."

"Do you know if Ricardo has a cousin named Carlo?"

"Yes. He visited us right after we were married. We were living in the art studio then. He looked just like Ricardo only the white streak in his hair was more prominent."

Deedra sighed. "Is it possible the man you call Ricardo is really Carlo?"

Sharlee started. "I kept asking if he really was Ricardo because he had changed so drastically. Then he and Hannah said I was imagining things and began to treat me as if I had some kind of mental problem. After that, they told people that I was ill, very frail, and that I didn't see people anymore."

They heard sounds on the stairs. Sharlee quickly shoved Deedra under the bed and lay down on it, her hand over her eyes when Hannah entered the room. Her manner was that of suspicion, her eyes darted about the room as if she expected to find something strange there.

"What's the matter? Are you sick?" Hannah demanded.

Sharlee sat up. "No."

"Where's the baby?"

"Asleep in his crib."

Deedra heard Hannah stomp away, evidently to

check on the child. Presently she returned. "Yes, he's still sleeping." Hannah seemed undecided about something. Deedra heard a twinge of doubt in her voice. She roamed about the room for a few minutes. "I'll bring your supper up in a few minutes."

With that she left.

Deedra could hear her stomping down the stairs.

Suddenly, Ricardo was in the room. He obviously moved about quietly, stealthily. "Do you have a headache?"

Sharlee replied in a tense tone, "No. I'm just tired today."

"The boy is sleeping?"

"Yes." Deedra could hear the fear in her reply.

"Just see that you don't try to leave. It would rile me up considerably, and I have an unreasonable temper. The boy is perfectly safe unless you do something stupid."

Hannah returned with the baby's supper and they both stayed while Sharlee fed him. Hannah's voice was gentle and soothing toward the baby and Deedra realized that Hannah was fond of the child.

Ricardo/Carlo remained silent though he watched the baby and Sharlee closely. He then began roaming about the room as if he felt there was another presence there.

"This really is a spooky old place," he muttered,

"you can almost feel the ghosts here. No wonder it has the reputation of being haunted."

Ricardo watched as Hannah cleaned the baby's face. She then she took him into the other room to change his diaper.

SEVENTEEN

FROM THE GLIMPSE DEEDRA got of the baby, she thought he was probably the most handsome child she had ever seen. Just from his features and coloring it was obvious that he wasn't Ricardo's child. The Embusteros had large features, tall rangy bodies, and very dark complexions. And there was no way that anyone could call them handsome.

Deedra wondered what Ricardo/Carlo thought when he looked at the child. He hadn't seemed hostile to the baby when he watched him being fed and she concluded that he didn't have murderous plans for the baby.

"You must promise," Ricardo told Sharlee, "that if I let you take the child outside, that you won't try to run away again." His voice cut through the room like a sharp-edged knife.

After a moment he continued. "You are to start thinking of the child as yours and mine now. And if you are asked, you are to tell people that the baby is mine. Your baby's future depends on that. Do you understand?"

"I thought you said you didn't want the baby?" Sharlee challenged.

Ricardo/Carlo started. "That suited me at the time. Now, it is imperative that people think the child is mine. It also prevents people from trying to take the child away. I'm going to make Trent Kettering wish he had never visited Anthea Abbey!"

There was silence following this pronouncement. Deedra knew the pretend Ricardo had left the room. Since she didn't hear his footsteps going down the stairs she wondered if he was lingering on the landing, trying to overhear whatever conversation might follow his departure.

Sharlee didn't say anything, and presently Hannah took the baby's empty plate, and went downstairs.

When they had gone, Sharlee led Deedra up the winding stairs to the rooms under the eaves and quickly returned to the baby. Sharlee didn't use those attic rooms and they were full of spider webs. It was, however, the best hiding place for Deedra. There was a slit of a window overlooking the front lawns and the entrance gates. She peered out, hoping to see Deke or Nick.

Suddenly she heard Ricardo's voice. "I must warn you, Sharlee, that Tito may want to take your child. Don't let him pick him up. Tito won't give him back if you do."

"Oh, he won't get this baby!" Sharlee said, but there was panic in her voice.

Deedra couldn't see the fake Ricardo's evil smile, but was certain that Sharlee had and knew it terrified her.

"We'll see," he said as he went down the stairs. Even up under the eaves, Deedra could hear him humming or muttering in a tone of satisfaction.

When they heard Hannah call Ricardo/Carlo to supper, Deedra began a search of the upstairs rooms. She didn't find any trap doors or hidden passages.

The storm that had been predicted for the next day arrived in a flurry of wind and rain. Wind screamed and banged around the old abbey, and it was twice as loud in the attic rooms where Deedra was trying to find a comfortable place to relax. She huddled between the floor joists and studs finding it exceedingly uncomfortable. A jagged flash of lightning preceded the thunder that reverberated overhead. Strong wind seemed to summon ghosts as it whistled and flailed around the old abbey, shaking every shutter, and creating a moaning sound under the eaves. That moaning sound alone would make anyone think the abbey was haunted, Deedra mused. Indeed, she found herself peering into the dark areas, into the shadowy places where specters might lurk.

Sharlee brought up a few candles for Deedra and quickly retreated to her rooms below.

Deedra planned to hold a candle at the window in hope that Deke and Nick might be out there looking for her. From the time of day, Deedra knew she had been gone over ten hours now. They would surely be wondering and worrying.

As the wind howled about, it stirred up ancient dust. Deedra couldn't prevent the feeling that it also stirred up something just outside her line of vision... and shuddered. She peered about anxiously, knowing if someone were to say, "boo," to her she would surely have a screaming fit. Shivers of coldness invaded her body and she longed to join Sharlee in the warm rooms below. But she knew Hannah would sense when things were not quite right, and was perhaps even now on the stairs waiting and listening.

Deedra knew she would have to wait until midnight to make any attempt at escape, and she wasn't sure it would be successful. Any hope of them surviving an attempt was the fact that Deke and Nick knew where she was and could assist in a rescue. Deedra knew that she could escape simply by running out the front door even if it did alert Carlo and Hannah. But it would be an act of cowardice not to take Sharlee and the baby with her. And that was the problem. Sharlee was extremely fearful and might refuse to go. And the baby might cry at the wrong moment.

She waved a candle in front of the window for a few minutes. She then sat back and listened to the storm. It was an unusual one for that time of year, though everything was dry and in need of rain. For several minutes raindrops pelted the abbey as if trying to scrub it clean.

Deedra shuddered again as she peered into the gloom, imagining there was pernicious movement out there among those vine-entangled grounds. What a spooky old place, she mused. Too bad Hollywood hadn't discovered its gloomy aura. Making certain no lights gleamed from the grounds, and that there were no crawly creatures in the dark corners, she settled back and tried to get comfortable.

Later when Deedra was certain that Carlo and Hannah were not lingering about on the turret stairs, she crept down to Sharlee's rooms.

Hannah had delivered Sharlee's supper and Sharlee had saved a portion for Deedra. Sharlee told her that Hannah would be returning for the tray and to bid Sharlee goodnight. Sharlee told her that Ricardo/Carlo was very demanding about having his meals on time. He wanted food and plenty of it. Hannah, she said, would be busy in the kitchen for a time, always cleaning the kitchen area before returning to get Sharlee's tray.

"You were really in love with Ricardo?" Deedra found it difficult to believe.

"Ricardo was very romantic then. I didn't realize that he wanted money to help purchase and remodel this place. I had just broken up with Deke Thomas who said he wasn't going to marry me. I guess I was in an emotional mood and I was seeking security. I thought an older man would give that to me. Call it marrying on the rebound, if you like," Sharlee whispered.

"What caused the change in Ricardo?"

"I don't know. It was just after we moved into the abbey. I hate this place, you know. The change seemed to come overnight. One day he was himself, the next he had turned into a cruel, demanding man. It was as if he had suffered a personality change. It made me confused and angry. Then after Ricardo found out I had been meeting with Trent Kettering, he turned cold and sometimes vicious. He started refusing to let me talk to anyone who phoned and he sent Sandy Harris home in a fit of anger. She never returned and I never heard from her again. I sometimes think he would have killed me if it wasn't for the fact that someone has always been inquiring about me, wanting to talk to me."

"One of the people trying to get you out of here is Deke Thomas," Deedra said.

"Deke? How do you know Deke?"

"Deke and I work for the same newspaper. We've teamed up on several news stories."

"Are you and Deke in love?" Sharlee asked.

"Like you said, Sharlee, Deke isn't the marrying

kind. Tell me about Trent Kettering. How did you manage to get outside to meet him?"

"We lived in the art studio and still had some things there. I was allowed outside at that time. Trent just sneaked back onto the grounds after having been refused admittance by Ricardo. It was after Ricardo found out about Trent that he prevented me from going outside or making any phone calls."

"There are quite a few people wondering what has happened to you. Several influential people in Hollywood contacted my editor. That's why I'm up here, though Curt Ralston's disappearance is an added reason. I thought that Curt was hidden in the cellars, and when the Embusteros refused to allow anyone to search around here, I was convinced of it. Now I know Curt's body and Ricardo's skeleton are down there. Carlo might have committed murder."

"There's a skeleton in the cellars?"

"Yes. Tito referred to it as 'Da.' I'm certain it's Ricardo's."

"My God! That means that Carlo really is disguising himself as Ricardo. Carlo was always jealous. Now he has everything that was Ricardo's!"

"Shhh! We've got to think of a way of getting out of here. Do Carlo or Hannah ever go into town for supplies?"

"Hannah does. Carlo never seems to leave the

place. Hannah drives over that dirt road to the east of the abbey. She never goes into Bermondy."

"Hannah told me she is Ricardo's sister," Deedra remarked.

"No. Ricardo never had any sisters. He was an only child. Hannah was his first wife, the mother of Tito," Sharlee replied.

"Oh!" Deedra was silent a moment. "Do you think there would be a chance of our sneaking out the back door while they are eating supper?"

"Perhaps. They usually leave the back door open. It makes Tito angry when he finds it locked. He has broken the lock several times. He threw things around in the kitchen the last time he found it locked. Ricardo...I mean, Carlo...tried to calm him down. Tito hit him, knocked him to the floor. Since then, I don't think they lock the back door. They only keep that siren thing on at night."

"Is," Deedra asked, "that surveillance monitor just in the lab or does he have several planted about the house?"

"No, just in the lab where he spends most of his time."

"The rooms up here all have cameras in them?"

"No. Just the one where the baby sleeps and those by the front windows."

"You had better finish your supper. Hannah is going to be here soon."

Sharlee cleaned her plate. When Hannah arrived a few minutes later, the tray was placed where Hannah had instructed Sharlee to put it. Deedra was hidden under the bed again.

When Hannah entered, Sharlee asked, "Hannah, there's a boy from Bermondy that is missing. They showed his picture on TV. Isn't that the boy that used to deliver the newspaper here?"

"Perhaps. Why do you ask?" Hannah's voice was stern, challenging.

"Just something to talk about," Sharlee reverted to her hopeless voice again.

Hannah sighed. "Perhaps I can get…ah…Ricardo to let you take the child out in the back yard. He needs to get out in the sunshine now that he is trying to walk." Her tone of voice had changed. Hannah was apparently very fond of the child and that fact had probably saved the child's life.

"Would you, Hannah? The baby really needs to go outside."

Hannah murmured something unintelligible and went into the room where the baby was sleeping. When Hannah emerged from the room, Deedra saw the remnants of a smile on her face.

They heard her clunk her way down the stairs with the empty food tray.

"Do you think Hannah heard us talking?" Deedra whispered.

"No. She's used to hearing me recite lines from the movies I've been in. I do that to keep from going berserk. That was before Hannah persuaded Ricardo... ah...Carlo to get me a TV. The sound of other people's voices really helps me."

"Hannah isn't really mean to you then?"

"Not like...ah...Carlo, but I am more afraid of what Hannah might do. She likes the baby and if she gets angry with me she might kill me and take the child. Carlo wouldn't do that, and he knows that Hannah isn't afraid of him. Hannah could always send Tito after him. Tito gets out of hand, you know, and I think he is the only person Hannah is afraid of. Hannah doesn't quite know if Tito is going to obey her or not these days."

"Anything special that made Hannah afraid of Tito?"

"He sometimes gets loose in the house and goes about moaning and gurgling and crooning. Then Ri... Carlo gives him a shot of something that makes him fall asleep. When he does, Tito doesn't move for hours and hours. At first they could pull him down the hall, and put him in that porch off the kitchen, but since he has grown so big, they just let him sleep wherever he falls."

"When Tito awakens, is he angry?"

"No," Sharlee shook her head. "He just seems more confused than ever. Tito shakes his head and always wants water. Then Hannah shoos him outside. When Hannah goes on errands to get supplies, she encourages Tito to stay around the house. I think that's a way of keeping Carlo in line." Then Sharlee added, "If he is Carlo."

"I'm certain he's Carlo. That's why Tito goes around the house crooning and moaning. He's grieving for his father. Tito knows what happened to Ricardo, knows he's the skeleton in the cellar. I think Hannah and Carlo tranquilize Tito so that he forgets it for a while. Carlo is probably afraid of Tito, afraid that Hannah might turn Tito against him, and that's why Carlo stays in the lab most of the time. The fact that everyone in Bermondy has been searching for Curt Ralston also frightens Carlo. He either knows or suspects that Curt's body is down in the cellars with Tito."

In a few moments of quiet Deedra heard the baby's soft cry. Sharlee hurried into his room. Fortunately, Deedra had remained under the bed, for Hannah was suddenly there. She had not clomped her way up the stairs this time.

"So, he's awake," Hannah smiled. Through the open door Deedra could see the smile and realized that Hannah was a frustrated old woman whose only child, Tito, was anything but a comfort to her. Hannah had brought the baby fruit and cookies, possibly without Carlo's knowledge. Hannah seated the baby in the high chair and began feeding him. It was obvious, however, that the baby was afraid of her. Nevertheless he ate as she directed.

Deedra had expected to find Hannah jealous of the child. She was obviously fond of him, and perhaps planned to eventually take the child just as Sharlee feared.

Sharlee stood to one side watching. The baby did as Hannah instructed, then looked at Sharlee who nodded and smiled. It was evident that Sharlee feared the baby wouldn't do as Hannah commanded. Perhaps she even sensed that Hannah was planning to take the child and was afraid Hannah would order Tito to do away with her.

Deedra shuddered at the thought.

The baby wanted more food.

"Can't he have another helping, Hannah? He's growing so rapidly that he requires more food."

Hannah shook her head. "You know Ricardo's rule. He doesn't want either of you to gain weight. That way you can't gain enough strength to run away."

Sharlee sighed. "I don't see why he doesn't let me go. What good am I to him, stashed away in this old turret?"

"I sometimes wonder about that myself," Hannah said to Carlo who had suddenly appeared in the doorway.

"I see the boy has grown during these past few

weeks." Carlo gave no indication that he had over-heard their conversation, or that he was going to allow the baby more to eat. "Hannah tells me that you want to take the boy outside," he said. "We've talked about this before. I know that he needs the fresh air and sunshine. I think we can plan on letting you do that in the next week if nothing interferes. It would do those snoopy F.B.I. people good to see that the boy is healthy and able to play in the back yard. I want you to move the boy's crib in front of that window where anyone out there can see him."

"You've never allowed me to let the baby look out the window!" Sharlee sounded surprised.

"Now that so many people are unduly curious about what goes on here at the abbey, I want them to realize that we have a domestic life here. That you don't want to leave because you want the baby to remain with his father!" Carlo's laugh filled the room with a wicked echo.

EIGHTEEN

Aware that she could easily escape, but that Sharlee was afraid to try, caused Deedra deep frustration. Sharlee's hesitance about taking the baby away was understandable though foolish. Yet who could blame her? If they were recaptured it would mean death to all of them.

So Deedra crept back to the attic room under the eaves, knowing that chances of their escape were very slim. She waved the candle in front of the window for a few minutes and sat back to listen to the storm. It was unusually fierce, drenching the abbey in a deluge of rainwater that seemed to have no ending.

She held the candle in front of the window again, waving it back and forth while muttering a silent prayer that Deke and Nick would be out there watching.

Out in the dark, huddled near the front gates Deke and Nick did see the candle and knew that Deedra was inside the abbey.

"Why is she way up there?" Nick muttered.

"Probably hiding. If Ricardo knew she was in the

house she wouldn't have a candle to alert anyone," Deke answered.

They scuttled across the wide lawn and vanished into the foliage, hiding in the summerhouse.

Their passing through the front gates alerted Carlo who immediately threw open the front door and peered into the night. Carlo waited there for some time, watching and listening, but the storm was the only noise he heard.

Hannah appeared at his side. "I doubt anyone is out in this weather. It was probably one of those wild animals that live in the woods running for shelter."

Reluctantly, Carlo shut and locked the front door.

Sharlee stood on the turret steps, her heart pounding. She was certain that someone had entered the front gates. Deedra was now among the missing and there would be people out there looking for her.

"Why are you out of your room, Sharlee?" Hannah demanded.

"The storm noises are really scary. They cause a moaning sound up under the eaves. I heard you at the front door and thought something might be the matter."

"No, nothing is the matter. You just get back up there where you belong. And don't come down again tonight!" Carlo shouted.

Pretending to be hurt by his words, she went slowly

back up the stairs. Sharlee knew that Carlo probably wouldn't go up to the turret area again that night.

"Is the baby asleep?" Hannah inquired.

"Yes."

"Good night then," Hannah stomped down the hall after Carlo.

Once upstairs, Sharlee located an extra blanket and took it up to Deedra. They dared not talk, not knowing whether their conversations could somehow be overheard in the rooms below.

Deedra nodded her thanks and Sharlee got back to her rooms just moments before Hannah stomped up the stairs with hot chocolate.

Hannah handed Sharlee the cup of steaming cocoa and then immediately went to check on the baby. She lingered around the room as if she expected to find something out of place there.

"Hannah, you seem nervous," Sharlee said.

Deedra, huddled on the attic stairs, heard Hannah's reply.

"You must take Ricardo's warning seriously, Sharlee. Don't let Tito hold the baby. He would squeeze the life out of him without even meaning to. I am going to try to persuade Ricardo to allow you to go out on the front lawns where Tito isn't allowed to roam. That would accomplish his purpose, and keep the baby away from Tito."

"Was Tito your only child, Hannah?"

"What do you mean, my child?" Hannah answered in a flare of anger.

"It's obvious. Besides, Ricardo once told me he had a son that was born mentally challenged. You aren't really Ricardo's sister, are you?" Sharlee challenged.

From her listening post on the stairs, Deedra held her breath.

Hannah was silent for a few moments before answering. "No. How could I have had other children when Ricardo abandoned me like that? I must say he did pay for the boy's keep in that institution until Tito outgrew everyone there, and became difficult to manage. There was no one who could control him and Tito wanted to be with Ricardo."

"When did Ricardo divorce you?"

Hannah stared at Sharlee, malevolence darkening her eyes. "He didn't divorce me. He married all those other women, and it wasn't legal. I am still his only legal wife. He didn't want the public to see me. I know what I look like, I can see in the mirror, and have been called an old witch many times. But I was good enough for Ricardo when he was just getting started with his inventions. I owned a large old house with a full basement where he could tinker at whatever he wanted, and I went out and worked. I supported us, paid the expenses it took for his inventions. Now he owes me, and I am not going to let him forget it!"

"What happened to those other wives?"

Hannah stared at her, the look of malevolent resentment plain in her dark eyes. "They died. I don't know what killed them. But I do know that one of them was very ill. They were rich women and Ricardo needed money, more than I could possibly provide. We agreed that if I let him marry those women, that he would always provide for Tito and me. When the institution notified us that they couldn't keep Tito any longer, Ricardo said he would find a large place where Tito could be with us. That I could live with him and his new wife. At the time you weren't yet his wife. I kept Tito at my house, though it caused consternation among the neighbors. They were very glad when we moved away."

"In other words, you are the proper heir to this old abbey and the money that goes with it?"

Hannah stared at her again, this time an evil smile tugged at the corners of her mouth. "Yes."

The wind howled anew, shaking shutters and eaves about the old abbey. But since the building was stone and couldn't be budged, the wind just whined in frustration.

Finally, Hannah went downstairs. Sharlee watched her go and began to prepare for bed. If Hannah returned, Sharlee had to be doing something that was habit with her. She could dress quickly if the need arose.

Deedra retreated to the upper reaches and waved the candle in front of the window again. She wondered if it could be seen through the rain.

Sharlee and Hannah's conversation had completed the puzzle. Everything fell into place. If Carlo had arrived with Hannah, that meant that they had planned to kill Ricardo. And that Hannah was an accomplice to murder. But Sharlee had soon become pregnant, and that posed a threat to them. The real Ricardo wouldn't have turned a pregnant wife out, and that fact caused Carlo and Hannah to change their plans.

Though she dozed, Deedra didn't go into a deep sleep. She needed to stay alert, and it wasn't possible to really rest in that uncomfortable place with the storm venting its anger on the abbey. The rain poured down as if someone had turned on a faucet in the "sky lakes." Surely the men wouldn't be out in it looking for her. They would have to wait until the storm passed over. It was a long time before the wind stopped howling about the old structure. Deedra huddled into the blanket, hugging her knees. She was uncomfortable and chilled, her hands and feet were numb.

She finally settled down with her back against a floor joist, listening to the storm sounds, wondering why she was an investigative reporter. Why had she tried such a dangerous venture here? She had to admit that this time it wasn't for that front-page story. She truly wanted to help Sharlee and her baby. She became determined to help after seeing the surveillance set-up. It was such a monstrous thing to do to one's wife. Then she remembered it was Carlo's doing, not Ricardo's. That a terrible crime had been committed at the abbey was certain. It was another gruesome thing to add to its reputation, and, being a news reporter, she was bound by her very nature to follow up on that lead.

At dawn Deedra crept down to Sharlee's rooms. Sharlee was still asleep and Deedra continued down the turret stairs. She hid behind a heavy drapery that covered the front windows. Soon she heard a shuffling sound.

Suddenly Hannah was there peering up the turret stairs. Deedra hadn't heard Hannah clomping around and knew by this that the old woman could creep about when it suited her purpose. Hannah seemed undecided about something. She was obviously uneasy. She kept looking up toward Sharlee's rooms in a kind of watchful way as if she expected to see movement there. Hannah finally shook her head, and quietly went down the dark hall toward her room at the back of the house.

Deedra peered out the front window hoping for a glimpse of Deke and Nick, but there was no sign of them. She hadn't dared breathe while Hannah stood within a few feet of her. The old woman seemed to have antennae that detected unusual movements. Hannah was definitely spooked. She had either heard Deedra creep down the stairs or had glimpsed a flickering shadow. Maybe just knowing that people were looking around for the missing Curt Ralston had set Hannah's nerves on edge.

Deedra had to be extra cautious from now on, making certain she threw no shadows. She tried the front door. It was locked, of course. She knew from her talk with Chuck Preston that there was no way out of the second floor either. Sandy Harris' map indicated that only two doors led to the outside. That meant they would have to sneak past Hannah's room, go through the kitchen and out the back door. An almost impossible feat with Hannah on guard every minute. Deedra wondered if Hannah ever really slept.

The only other way out was through the trap door and into the cellars. That meant letting Tito see the baby. Would he try to take it away from them? And the smell of carrion down there was almost overwhelming. Sharlee was in no condition to see that skeleton, let alone the dead Curt Ralston. It had been almost more than Deedra could cope with, and she knew she would never again see rats without the memory of Tito squeezing or stomping them to death. She also realized she could never let anyone know how deeply the terror had affected her. Besides, investigative reporters were supposed to be tough. They couldn't allow things to throw them into a tizzy, especially if that reporter happened to be a woman. Deedra had the reputation of being a tough investigative reporter and she intended to keep it that way.

By the time Deedra returned to the turret, she was nervous, on edge, and shuddered with revulsion at contemplation that they might have to leave through the dungeons.

Sharlee and the baby were sleeping. What to do? Awaken them and leave by way of the trap door? Wait to see if they would be rescued? Unless Deke and Rex Walling were able to obtain a search warrant, that option didn't seem likely.

Before she could awaken them, Hannah stomped up the stairs.

Deedra barely had time to slide under Sharlee's bed.

Hannah peered at Sharlee and then went to the baby's crib. She smiled when she looked at him. Deedra thought it was the one thing Hannah did that renewed her membership in the human race.

But the opportunity to escape had vanished. They would have to wait until night again. Deedra almost groaned at the prospect. She was hungry and dirty, and wanted to sleep in a comfortable bed.

Before Hannah left, Carlo appeared at the door.

"Why are you up here so early, Hannah?" he demanded.

"The storm kept me awake. I was uneasy about Sharlee. I thought there was something amiss, but obviously there isn't."

At the sound of their voices, Sharlee awoke. "What is it?" she asked sleepily.

"Nothing. Just go back to sleep. I was checking on the baby." Hannah waved Carlo down the stairs in front of her.

They heard Hannah ask Carlo if he wanted her to make fresh coffee.

Deedra thought they went to the kitchen.

"We'll have to wait until tonight now," Deedra whispered. "I'm going to have trouble avoiding Hannah."

"Go over to the second floor stairs and up to one of the rooms there. Hannah seldom goes there. You can stay out of sight there if you don't make any noise."

Sharlee handed her a box of cookies and a can of soda.

Deedra scuttled up the stairs leading to the second floor. Passing the main hall she heard the murmur of voices from the kitchen area. Quickly, she mounted the stairs and set about finding a room with a comfortable bed. Though she planned to only lie down for a minute, she was soon deeply asleep.

OUT IN THE SUMMERHOUSE, Deke and Nick were at a loss about what to do. They hadn't seen the waving candlelight for some time, and they had missed seeing Deedra at the front window. They took turns on guard, while one slept the other watched for Carlo or Hannah. They were certain they wouldn't venture out in the wet drizzle left by the storm unless they saw someone on the grounds. From the waving candlelight they had concluded that Deedra was inside and had so far evaded capture. Both men were fully aware that getting her out might prove difficult…if not disastrous.

NINETEEN

DEEDRA AWOKE LATE IN the afternoon. The cookies Sharlee had provided scarcely quenched her gnawing hunger. There were sounds from Carlo's lab located just below the room and it was the noises made by him that had awakened her. A bathroom adjoined the bedroom. She used it though she had to remember not to flush the toilet. She didn't want to alert Carlo that someone was upstairs.

There wasn't a whole hell of a lot to do to while away the time. She tried to think of escape plans, knowing they would have to make an attempt tonight or she would have to leave by herself and try to rescue Sharlee later. And the only way of even having a chance to escape was out through the cellar where no alarms rang and the Embusteros would ignore any noise they made.

Hannah chose that day to drive off for supplies. She went up to say goodbye to Sharlee, and look at the baby before she left.

Sharlee stood on the stairs and watched her leave the house. Since she drove out on the road to the east, Deedra was able to watch her drive away also. Hannah had changed her flowing black dress for something more appropriate. Now Deedra knew why no one had seen a woman of her description, of an old witch woman wearing a long black dress. A woman with a long nose. What was Hannah's purpose in wearing that long black dress? Did it have a special meaning for her or for Tito? Was it something she wore to control Tito? It certainly looked uncomfortable, but it did resemble the habits of nuns confined to cloisters in the middle ages. Perhaps Tito had been institutionalized in a convent where nuns still wore the old style habits.

She heard Carlo moving about. Once, he went to the turret stairs and called up to Sharlee. When she answered he said, "Just checking. Hannah should be back soon. What are you doing?"

"I'm watching television. Do you think I can take the baby outside today?"

"Don't be silly, it's far too damp after that rain."

It was difficult to spend the whole day on the second floor with nothing to do. To keep from making noise, she lay on the bed and thought about her life, knowing that Deke would never marry her. Even if he were upset about her now, he would revert to his "not marrying" stance once this crisis was over. It was definitely the time to start looking for someone else if she ever expected to raise a family. Despite the fact that she was in love with Deke, she couldn't wait on him forever. Damn it all, anyway! Deedra knew that men were put off by her aggressive ways, but investigative reporters were aggressive, that was part of what it took. Though Deke did admire her adventurous spirit, did think of her as rather courageous, he probably preferred the more feminine type.

Eventually her thoughts went back to her present predicament. Surely there was a way they could escape this awful place. But with all her pondering, Deedra didn't arrive at an alternative that would keep them from having to go out through the dungeons.

Later that afternoon the alarm rang, alerting them that someone had entered through the front gates. Deedra heard Carlo hurry toward the front door.

She crept to the top of the stairs, hiding in the shadows cast by the banisters.

Deke's voice sent a thrill of excitement through her. Did Deke have the sheriff with him? Was he there to rescue them?

"My name is Deke Thomas, I'm a reporter for the *Daily Spokesman*. I believe you gave an interview to a colleague of mine several days ago. Well, she's turned up missing, and we wondered if by chance she had visited out here again?"

Carlo was obviously taken aback. "Why, no. I haven't seen her. Did she say she was going to visit again?"

"No. We're just checking everywhere. You probably

know that the newspaper delivery boy is missing, and now she is, too. It's very strange, and very frightening. The townspeople are becoming alarmed."

This silenced Carlo for a moment. "I haven't seen her since she delivered that newspaper article she wrote about me. The last time she was here she poked about the grounds, said she was out looking for the missing boy. You may look around if you like."

"Thank you." Deke went down the stairs and joined Nick in the driveway. They went off toward the overgrown garden. It was Deke's and Nick's way to let Deedra know that they knew she was inside the abbey, and somewhere near should she need them.

Carlo watched them through a downstairs window.

Deedra knew that Deke and Nick's presence had put the fear into Carlo. He muttered something unintelligible that sounded like cursing. He was definitely agitated.

Sharlee watched the men from the upstairs window. Knowing that Carlo also watched, she didn't attempt to wave at them.

When at last Deke and Nick drove away, Carlo shouted up to Sharlee. "Have you seen that reporter woman?"

"You mean that young woman that visited you to get a story on your inventions?" Sharlee asked.

"Yes."

"I haven't seen her today. And I've been watching out the window."

This answer evidently satisfied Carlo for he went back to his lab muttering something about the missing boy and Tito.

It was too dangerous for Deedra to return to the turret rooms and she needed to hear what Hannah and Carlo said when Hannah returned. From her hiding place she could hear them. From the attic rooms she couldn't. From the second floor she could witness Hannah's return.

The sound of a car engine alerted Deedra to Hannah's return. Deedra saw her clomping across the side lawn. She heard the back door slam and Hannah's approach to the turret rooms to check on Sharlee and the baby. Satisfied that everything was as she had left it, Hannah carried in the supplies. She didn't ask Carlo to help her and he didn't offer.

When she had carried in the last package Carlo said, "Two men were here looking for that reporter woman. They say she is missing just like that newspaper delivery boy. I want you to check the cellars and see if Tito has her down there. It would be just like him to grab her and take her down to those caverns. Heaven knows what he would do with a woman down there."

"If you want to check the cellars for her, you do it. I am not putting my life in danger by going down there with Tito. He is already upset about being kept there. He's lonesome now, and that makes him very dangerous. Ricardo was unwise to try to change him like that. We are going to have to make a decision about him soon. He could get loose and kill someone, then there would be all kinds of trouble and investigation…and you, Carlo, would end up in prison."

"I'm not going down there," Carlo replied, "You know how Tito hates me. You are right, however, a decision has to be made about him…and soon."

There was silence while they stared at each other. Finally, Carlo went back to the lab. The sound of the door slamming showed his displeasure.

Deedra felt a sense of satisfaction in knowing that her theory about Ricardo/Carlo had been right. That didn't help her present predicament, but it made it more imperative than ever to get Sharlee and the baby away. Obviously Hannah and Carlo were planning to dispose of Tito. They just hadn't planned on how to do it yet. She was certain that Hannah knew that Tito had captured Curt Ralston and had killed him and that was probably Hannah's basis of fear now. With Tito upset, Hannah was afraid to go into the cellars with him, afraid Tito might kill her in a fit of rage.

It seemed years until dusk. Deedra knew they would have to try to get out that night. There could be no postponing it now. Sharlee would just have to make the effort despite her frail strength. She hoped that

Carlo had forgotten to lock the front door after Deke's visit. It would certainly simplify matters. Trying to go out the kitchen door was suicidal with Hannah constantly on the prowl. Deedra had to acknowledge the fact that they would have to go out through the cellars, and she was going to have to placate Tito to allow that to happen. If she'd had the gun with her, things would have been simpler. She would have shot Hannah and Carlo if necessary. Without it, Hannah could just grab the baby. Then Sharlee would never leave. But just the thought of another trip through the cellars caused her quaking terror.

For something to do, Deedra investigated every room on that floor. She saw the room that Chuck Preston had stayed in on his fateful visit here. She recalled Chuck saying that there were ghostlike images floating about in the hallway and knew now that they weren't put into operation unless someone was on the second floor. Though she made a cursory search, she didn't find whatever it was that put them into motion. The rooms were empty, of course. A few had beds and dressers in them and some showed signs of the remodeling effort. A few had new paint and bathroom fixtures.

Near suppertime, she crept back to her hiding place in the shadows of the second floor landing and waited.

Presently Hannah went up the turret stairs

carrying a tray. The faint sound of their voices floated downward.

Carlo suddenly appeared at the foot of the turret stairs and stood there listening, a look of malevolence straining his features. What was he planning? Was Hannah in danger, too? She was, after all, the real heir to the property and all of Ricardo's money. Did Carlo think they would share equally, or did he want it all? With Tito gone, Hannah wouldn't have a hold over Carlo. Had Hannah thought of that? Carlo could keep Sharlee and the baby indefinitely, at least until it was time for the boy to go to school. He could solve that by sending them both "away" at the same time. Who would miss them? People would stop trying to get in touch with Sharlee after a few years, and Carlo could say that she died in some other town and that the boy was in boarding school. Surely Hannah must have sensed her precarious position, must have suspected what was in Carlo's mind.

Carlo remained at the foot of the stairs until he heard Hannah's stomping stride, then quickly vanished down the dark hall toward the lab.

Hannah clomped down the stairs, looked about in a suspicious way and strode down the hall toward the kitchen.

There was the sound of the kitchen door being opened and Hannah's shout, "Get out of here, Tito!

I put your supper out there. You just get out of here now!"

There was a gurgled mutter, almost like a curse, then the back door slammed.

She heard Hannah say, "We've got to do something about that Tito. He's just too big to handle anymore."

The smell of the food caused Deedra's stomach to rumble in protest. She hoped Sharlee would save her something from her tray. Deedra knew that hunger would drive her out of the abbey if nothing else did. She simply refused to stay there and starve for Sharlee. She then began to wonder if she had wasted her efforts trying to rescue her. Wouldn't it be ironic if Sharlee refused to go? What if they had such mind control over her she was afraid to leave? Deedra knew that battered wives often didn't leave dangerous situations because of a dominance and fear factor.

The evening dragged on. She could hear the sounds of Sharlee's TV, and another TV she thought was located in Hannah's room. She didn't know where Carlo was, didn't dare move from her hiding place lest he be in the shadows of the dark hallway. And he did appear at sudden intervals when he stood at the foot of the turret stairs listening.

Carlo was obviously anxious and she reckoned Deke's visit had caused it. But she sensed there was something else, something wicked, going on in his mind. Did Carlo have romantic plans for Sharlee? He was, after all, posing as her husband and perhaps thought he should take over the marital privileges. Did Sharlee sense that?

Obviously Hannah and Carlo didn't trust each other out of immediate sight. Carlo might have no compunction about getting rid of Hannah if he thought he could get away with it. But Hannah was as dangerous in her way as was Carlo, perhaps even more dangerous. She could send Tito to kill Carlo. There was all that money and property at stake. Hannah probably didn't want to share with Carlo and she had Tito to provide for. She could kill Carlo and dispose of his body in the cellars long enough for the rats to reduce him to a skeleton that no one could recognize. Then simply get rid of the bones. Hannah wouldn't want two Ricardos around, and if by chance the skeletons were discovered, Hannah could blame it on Tito. Who could prove differently, since Tito had obviously killed Curt Ralston? There were infinite ways for Hannah to kill Carlo, have Tito shove him over the ledge into the ravine for one. Was that what Hannah had been thinking when she stared into the canyon the other day?

Deedra guessed they both hesitated to take action because of the repercussions, the fact that everyone was hunting for the missing Curt Ralston, and now for her. They had no way of knowing what the F.B.I.

people might do. So they probably wouldn't take any action for the next few hours, unless something caused Tito or Hannah to lose their temper...or if Carlo suspected he would lose everything if he didn't act quickly.

At last night settled in. Hannah made another trip up the turret stairs. Carlo checked to make certain the front door was locked and put the siren in operation. After a few minutes lights went out at the back of the house. A waiting silence hovered.

It was fortunate that Deedra hadn't moved from her hiding place behind the banisters because Carlo crept down the hall and stood at the foot of the turret stairs listening. He seemed indecisive about something and Deedra felt a quiver of fear for Sharlee. After a few minutes Carlo went down the hall toward Hannah's room, disappearing into the shadows. Deedra didn't see him again and didn't know whether he went into his room or not.

When there had been silence for several hours, Deedra crept down the second floor stairs, across the hall and up the turret stairs.

Sharlee and the baby were both awake.

"Quick, you have to pack a few things for the baby and a jacket for yourself. I heard it start to rain again."

Even as she spoke the wind whipped and whined

around the old turret. Cold drafts scuttled along the floors.

"This old place could easily be haunted with its cold drafts scuffing across the floors like the wafting of ghosts!" Deedra whispered.

Sharlee nodded, hesitating about getting the baby ready, causing Deedra a new surge of fear. Was Sharlee going to refuse to go now?

"Sharlee, if you're not going with me, you need to write out a plea to a judge telling him you are being held here against your wishes, so that a warrant can be issued. Otherwise, there's nothing anyone can do for you and the baby." When Sharlee didn't answer, "Sharlee, you have to make up your mind. I can't stay here and starve to death waiting for you to make up your mind! I need to get out, and if you won't leave, then I'll have to go alone."

"I don't think I can carry the baby that far," Sharlee whispered.

"I'll carry him. You just need to get yourself out. Now, what do you want to do?"

Sharlee couldn't decide. She was afraid they wouldn't get away, afraid that Carlo or Tito would take the child from her.

"Listen carefully," Deedra hissed. "Carlo can take the baby away from you any time he wants to. There isn't anything to prevent him from doing that. You aren't strong enough to fight him. Even though

Hannah is fond of the child, she would be forced to make a decision. It wouldn't be in your favor either. I don't have much time. You've got to make up your mind whether you want me to take you out of here, or if you want me to take a letter to the judge so a warrant can be issued that will allow the sheriff to get you."

Sharlee, terrified and uncertain, still hesitated. She had been so put down and humiliated that she lacked the confidence to make decisions.

The storm sounds increased. Strong gusts shook the eave troughs, clattering and shaking the vines growing at the side of the turret.

Among the wind noises, Deedra suddenly detected another and quickly scooted under the bed.

Hannah appeared in the doorway. "Oh, you're awake."

"Yes. The storm noises woke me. It's loud here in the turret."

Hannah took a turn around the room and went to look at the baby who had fallen asleep again. Hannah seemed disturbed, definitely anxious and evidently suspicious. "Sharlee, did you see that reporter person out of the window either today or yesterday?"

"No. I didn't. I don't always look out the window though, and it's been raining. I wouldn't think anyone would be out in it. Why do you ask?"

"I heard she was missing," Hannah replied. "Did

you see those two men that came to the house earlier today?"

"Yes. What did they want?"

Hannah stared at her for a moment. "They told Ricardo about the missing newspaper reporter. They thought she might have returned here. You didn't see her on the lawns or over by the road, did you?"

"No, I only saw those two men. One of them looked familiar," Sharlee replied.

Evidently that was something Hannah didn't want to talk about. She went to the medicine cabinet in Sharlee's bathroom and brought a sleeping pill and a glass of water to Sharlee. "You need to get some rest. Take this sleeping pill and you'll sleep through the noise of that old storm."

Sharlee hesitated, and then pretended to take the pill. She crawled into bed.

Hannah strode to the door. "I shall bring your breakfast up at the usual time, you should sleep until then."

"Yes. Thank you."

Hannah stomped away; they could hear her going down the stairs. Then there was the sound of voices. They knew that Carlo had been waiting at the foot of the stairs for Hannah.

"Don't those people ever sleep?" Deedra hissed at Sharlee.

"They always check. It's a good thing I didn't have anything packed. Hannah is suspicious."

"I doubt she will check anymore tonight. She gave you that sleeping pill so she wouldn't have to," Deedra replied.

"Let's get out of here. Just hearing that Deke Thomas checked to find out if you were here and didn't learn anything means they weren't able to get a warrant. I don't think Carlo will ever let me go. I'm just afraid we're going to get caught leaving. I'm afraid of Tito. I keep thinking that he might kill my baby. If he killed Curt Ralston, he could just as easily kill my baby!"

"It's a chance we have to take. If you decide to stay, then I'm getting out of here. Just tell me what you want to do," Deedra whispered.

"Let's go." Sharlee finally decided, though Deedra knew she was extremely frightened.

Quickly and as quietly as possible, Sharlee packed a few things for the baby.

"Be sure to take his pacifier. We don't dare let him cry," Deedra reminded. "I heard Carlo check the lock on the front door. It only opens with that special key he carries, so we have to go out through the cellars since Hannah is on guard near the back door."

When Sharlee nodded she said, "Let me see if anyone is lurking in the hall." Deedra quietly left the room.

The hall was dark and no lights showed from the back of the house. Deedra stood very still and listened. Her inner voice told her that no one lingered in the darkness below. She returned to Sharlee's room.

"Ready? Pick up the baby and put the pacifier in his mouth," she instructed Sharlee.

TWENTY

THEY CREPT DOWN THE STAIRS, Deedra carrying
the baby. They paused in the hall. When they heard
no sounds of movement and saw no lights suddenly
turned on, they proceeded to the trap door where
Deedra handed the baby to Sharlee.

Fortunately, the trap door opened with scarcely a
sound.

Beside her, Sharlee gasped in surprise.

By Tito's candle light, Deedra could make out the
table, still placed beneath the trap door. She could
hear Tito snoring. He didn't move, nor did the rhythm
of his breathing change. Deedra lowered herself to
the table and took the baby from Sharlee. She carefully placed him on the table in order to help Sharlee
down.

The baby fussed.

Sharlee gasped.

"Hurry," Deedra hissed.

Sharlee finally got down through the door. Deedra
practically had to lift her, the old chair threatening
to give way under her. "Get down, and pick up the
baby!"

Finally Sharlee did as she was told and Deedra was able to push the trap door shut. This time it made a screeching sound that woke Tito.

He stared at Deedra a moment, the candle light making his eyes seem large and protruding.

Deedra spoke to him. "Tito, you come with us, we are going to take you away from here. You want to go away, don't you? You want to get away from the rats!"

For the space of an eternity Tito stared at them, flexing his hands as if in readiness to grasp and squeeze. Then he nodded.

"Get over here beside me," Deedra told Sharlee. "Hold the baby close to you." Then she beckoned Tito. "Follow me, Tito. I am your friend. I am going to take you away from here, away from the rats."

Tito gurgled something that might have been "all right," though she wasn't at all sure that he even understood her.

Deedra held Tito's candle and led the way through the dank caverns where rats scurried along ahead of them. Sharlee screamed out loud from time to time. As they approached the caverns closest to the back entrance, the smell became more pronounced. Although it didn't seem as overwhelming as it had been when Deedra had been in the cellars earlier. The rats had taken care of that. They reached the cavern containing the skeleton and Deedra saw what was left of Curt's body lying alongside the trundle that held the skeleton of Ricardo Embustero. Rats had eaten all the flesh away from Curt's body.

Deedra shuddered.

Then she gestured to Tito. "Pick the boy up and bring him with us."

At first Tito didn't respond. He just stared at her, flexing his over-large fists.

"Tito! Pick up the boy, and bring him with us! We are going out to meet friends. Friends who will take you away from the rats."

It took all Deedra's courage to stare Tito down, to prevent him from seeing her fear, and to calm him. Her breathing was shallow, her heart thumping.

Tito flexed his hands and nodded. He mumbled something.

"You bring the boy with us, Tito! Don't leave him down here with the rats!" Deedra commanded.

Tito hurried to obey her, awkwardly grabbing up what was left of the boy's wasted body. He then strode ahead of them.

Deedra took the baby from Sharlee. "Don't faint now, we've got to get out of these cellars!"

Sharlee merely groaned, and stumbled along after her.

When they reached the stairs leading to the outside door, Tito stood there blocking the way, Curt's body dangling from his arms. They couldn't get past him. He stared at the baby who had begun to whimper.

Deedra quickly covered the baby's head with a blanket.

A rat ran across the floor. Suddenly Tito burst into vicious swearing, words that were understood by both Deedra and Sharlee. He then he stomped the rat to death.

Sharlee vomited.

This brought other rats that quickly consumed the vomit and the squished remains of the rat.

"Oh!" Sharlee wobbled on her feet.

"Don't faint! We have to get out of here." Deedra hissed. "Go on up the stairs, Tito. You did good killing that rat! Now, Tito, open the door so we can take you away from here, away from the rats!"

Tito nodded, and pushed the door open.

Fresh air brushed their faces with a gentleness that steadied Deedra's frazzled nerves.

For a moment Tito stood in the doorway looking about. Daylight was just beginning. For a minute, Deedra thought Tito was going to change his mind. He backed down the steps and looked at Deedra, and then at the baby she carried.

Sharlee gasped in fear.

With that, Tito led them out of the cellars.

Deedra, still carrying the baby, hurried them across the back yard, then down the trail at the side of the ravine. This seemed to please Tito, who smiled and helped Sharlee when she seemed to lose her footing.

Sharlee emitted a faint scream each time Tito touched her, but since Deedra was carrying the baby, she followed along without protest.

The trail was a slippery, muddy mess from the rain and the way was long and treacherous. Before they reached the other side, Deedra was exhausted. She hadn't eaten for many hours. She was weary and very thirsty and the relief of getting out of those dank cellars nearly overwhelmed her.

After slipping and sliding along the trail over the landslide, they had reached the far side. Deedra looked back in time to see Carlo searching the back yard. Evidently he had noted that the cellar door was open. Carlo looked across the ravine and saw them. A malicious snarl creased his face, but he made no attempt to follow, knowing that Tito would kill him. Carlo made one final fist shake at them and disappeared back into the abbey.

Despite the fact that it was just daylight, and even though it had rained in the night, it was already turning warm. They had to rest in the shade of trees until Sharlee could get her breath. Sharlee hadn't exercised in months and was pitifully weak. The climb had taken all her strength. She wouldn't have been able to cross over that landslide if Tito hadn't helped her.

Deedra stood up. "Let's hope my car is still parked where I left it."

The baby fretted, and Sharlee gave him a bottle.

Tito watched in fascination, never once letting the body of Curt Ralston slip from his grasp.

"See, Tito," Deedra said to reassure him, "this is how we feed the baby. We are going to take you where you are going to be fed every day. And not dog food, either!"

Tito nodded as if he understood. He seemed to have lost his fierceness and Deedra guessed just getting him away from the rats calmed him. Who wouldn't be driven to the brink having to live in those awful cellars?

Sharlee had developed a severe headache from all the exertion. When she saw Deke and Nick hurrying across the field toward them she thought the headache had given her hallucinations. But suddenly the men were there.

"Deke!" Sharlee nearly fainted with the relief.

Deke picked her up and carried her toward his car.

Deedra felt rejected. Deke hadn't said a word to her.

Nick took the baby from her, and Deedra was left to lead Tito toward her car. He was still carrying Curt Ralston's body. When they reached her car and

Deedra urged him to get inside, Tito looked uncertain as if he was about to turn back.

"It's all right, Tito. I'm going to take you away from the rats. If you stay here Carlo and Hannah will make you go back down in the cellar."

Tito stared at her, then smiled. After she smiled back at him, he got into the back seat of her car. He did not put the remnants of Curt's body down.

Deke and Nick had put Sharlee and the baby in Deke's car and stood in awe as they watched Deedra lead Tito to her car and persuade him to get in.

"Just take Sharlee and the baby and go into town. I'll follow with Tito...and Curt Ralston's body," Deedra ordered.

Nick looked as if he was going to be sick. Deke obviously didn't like the idea of her being alone with Tito.

Deedra threw them a crooked smile, a smile she didn't feel. "It's all right. Tito and I are friends. I am taking him away from those awful rats!"

Tito smiled at them and even though Deke didn't understand the reference to "the rats," he understood that Deedra had the situation under control.

It was a ride Deedra would never forget, nor want to live through again. It was grotesque. She was transporting in her new car a happy mutant hugging a dead boy's skeleton who was gleeful because he was getting away from the rats.

They drove directly to the newspaper where the F.B.I. men were waiting. They stared in disbelief as Deedra opened the door for Tito. He got out with the boy's skeleton in his arms, a smiling giant youth holding the skeleton of another boy as gently as he could.

Deedra took Tito by the arm and led him over to the F.B.I. men.

"This is Tito. He found Curt Ralston on the abbey property. And being very lonesome and having to live in the cellars, he took Curt down into the caverns with him. He only meant to be friends, and didn't realize his strength. He is very fond of Curt, but he hugged him so tight he broke his neck. Then the rats got to him."

At the word *rats,* Tito made angry gurgling sounds.

"Now, Tito needs a good home, a place where there are no rats, and where he is fed properly. I think if you ask him politely, he will give you Curt's body and go with you."

Tito handed Curt over to the men, proving to Deedra that he was not nearly as clueless as Hannah would like to pretend.

"Now, if someone doesn't give me a cup of coffee, I'm going to have a screaming fit right here in the street!" Deedra demanded.

The F.B.I. men took charge of Tito and Curt

Ralston. Deke and Nick escorted her into the newspaper office where Sharlee was sitting in a chair holding the baby, and in the throes of quiet hysterics.

Fortunately there had only been a few people on the sidewalk when they returned with their grisly cargo, and the F.B.I. men quickly sent them on their way.

Deedra was handed a cup of coffee and a doughnut. She sank into one of R.D.'s more comfortable chairs. When she had recovered enough to phone Clete Bailey, the men listened quietly as she told of her adventures.

Meanwhile, the sheriff had obtained a warrant to search the abbey. Carlo and Hannah were arrested after the skeleton of Ricardo Embustero was found in the cellar. Hannah identified it as the real Ricardo, and never changed her claim that it was Carlo who had killed him.

Deke went to the restaurant up the street and bought Deedra a hamburger, fries, and a large chocolate milk shake. Deedra was certain she had never eaten anything more delicious. Deke had done the thing that helped her regain her sense of self. By the time Chuck Preston arrived, having heard the news via Clete Bailey, Deedra was smiling, almost able to put the gruesome events out of her mind.

"Another scoop, eh, Deedra? I wouldn't have gone

down in those cellars for anything," Chuck smiled his admiration.

Trent Kettering arrived and took Sharlee and the baby away. No one really knew where they went, though several days later Sharlee called Deedra from Trent's home in Hollywood to thank her for rescuing them.

Nick had already gone back north and the only thing they heard from him was a statement of charges sent to Clete Bailey at the newspaper. It arrived several days later, and Nick had enclosed a note of apology to Deedra for not having been the one to rescue her.

No one at the newspaper ever learned what arrangements the F.B.I. made for Tito. It was as if he had vanished from this planet.

Deke and Deedra resumed their non-marrying status, dating occasionally, with Deedra more determined than ever to find someone who did want to actually marry her.

Deedra was occasionally bothered by nightmares in which rats seemed to scuttle about. She would awaken covered with perspiration. She never tried to tell anyone about it, knowing that the adventures she met and faced were all part of being an investigative reporter. Besides, she had the reputation of being tough, and she didn't want anyone to know that she really wasn't.

REQUEST YOUR FREE BOOKS!

2 FREE NOVELS
PLUS 2 FREE GIFTS!

WORLDWIDE LIBRARY®
MYSTERY
™
Your Partner in Crime

WWL10